ALWAYS CRASHING

ISSUE FIVE

CHICAGO, ILLINOIS • PITTSBURGH, PENNSYLVANIA

ISBN: 978-0-578-29039-3

Always Crashing is a magazine of fiction, poetry, and nameless things around and in-between. We publish one print issue per year and feature online content year-round. We are headquartered in Chicago, Illinois, and Pittsburgh, Pennsylvania.

Editors: Jessica Berger & James Tadd Adcox

Managing Editor: Helenmary Sheridan

The editors wish to thank Matthew Kosinski, Gesina Phillips, Emily Kiernan, and Elayne Sheridan for their generous support.

For submission guidelines, ordering information, and access to our electronic edition featuring new work every two weeks, please visit www.alwayscrashing.com

SIDE A

SIDE B

/ side a

THE BESTIARY OF INCOMPLETE MONSTERS

/ Lillie E. Franks

THE CENTAUR

The horse is a frightened and fragile animal. It meets the world at top speed, racing the other direction. But the horse's rider is brave and bloody. He offers himself to death for a thousand different reasons, none of which are good enough.

All it takes is a strange sound or a second thought to put the centaur to the test. Immediately, the head turns towards the danger. "To face fear is strength and strength is good," or else "I am more afraid of fear than of what frightens me." But the horse cannot understand words. The horse only understands danger and speed.

It must end in violence. One half must hurt the other enough to turn it around or they will tear themselves apart. Whatever must end in violence is a monster.

The centaur is the monster of fear.

THE CHIMERA

The lion and the goat are different, profoundly different, but the serpents' venom runs through both the same. I would, if it were possible, record every singularity of these two creatures combined, but it is always the serpent who triumphs, always the serpent who, in anger or in fear, destroys both of its fellows. All I can say about the lion and the goat is that they thrash differently when they feel the pang of poison in their hearts. But that is not a difference; it is the memory of a difference, and a bitter memory at that.

Still, the lion thrashes angrily, with large, sweeping movements, as if it also knows it deserves better. The goat dies quietly, perhaps a quiet of dignity or maybe just of habit.

The chimera is the monster of death.

THE MYRMECOLEON

The myrmecoleon has the body of a lion and the head of an ant. It was said by early bestiaries that the head, following its instinct, would eat grains, while the body, whose stomach was used to meats, would starve. But this claim was made by authors who had not seen the creature, who imagined it only by its absence. More, it was made by authors who had no pity for the creature, and could only imagine it dead.

In truth, what happens is quite different. The ant head, knowing its body needs meat to survive, hunts and kills. It even goes so far as to eat, even though meat is strange and disgusting to it. If you told the myrmecoleon that eating can be pleasant and joyful, it would laugh at you, because it only knows eating as a sad necessity.

This is the first of the differences between the head and the body. The body needs; the head searches.

The myrmecoleon is the monster of need, which is to say, desire.

THE MINOTAUR

In the minotaur, the human appears again, but as a body, not a head. If the nature of a human's head is to choose to face danger, to be bold and resolute, then the nature of its body is to want the things that come only with danger. Together, they are one whole creature. They are a not-monster, a life.

The minotaur's head is not a tool for taking the fruits of danger. It is a weapon that destroys. Where its body is in desperate need of possibilities, of the beautiful things that come with stepping out onto bridges that might fall, its head can buy it only one, and that is safety. It is a lonely and murderous safety, but to a head that can only imagine safety and death, it is enough. Meanwhile, the body sickens with an illness its head cannot understand.

The people gored by its horns would pity it if they knew, and I don't know if it would save them.

The minotaur is the monster of anger.

THE UNKNOWN

I must include myself somewhere in this book or it would be incomplete, and I refuse to produce something that is incomplete. You don't have to ask my why not, do you? It is incomplete things that attach themselves to other incomplete things which do not fit them and become monsters.

A monster is a combination of pieces. It is not the pieces that are monstrous, but the way they are joined.

And yes, a monster must end in violence. The pieces must be separated from each other. If one piece is the head and the other the body, what does that change? Nothing, except to the monster, which is to say to no one.

I must include myself in this book, but I don't know the parts I'm made of, only the strange and awful whole. It is a monstrous whole, I know, for I hate it and so do the people who look on my face and are filled with fear. But where I am divided, and into what, I cannot tell you.

Instead, I will say only what I can, which is that there is one more monster than all the others I have recorded. It lives by the river, and it is the monster of me, myself, which is to say, the unknown.

And someday, it too must be destroyed.

THE CYCLOPS

The Cyclops is complete and incomplete, and this is enough to make it monstrous. It should have an eye, but it doesn't. Perhaps it is the fear of what it might fill this lack with that makes it hateful.

If you join yourself to the wrong piece, you will become a monster. If you do not find a second piece at all, you will still be monstrous.

This is the trap.

Sometimes even hope isn't good enough. Somedays I look at my face reflected in the rushing waters and wonder what pieces might still be missing.

THE DRAGON

But there is hope. There is another way.

There is a dragon.

I do not know the pieces of the dragon either. Maybe they are subtler, hidden underneath the skin as mine are. Maybe the dragon itself is only one piece, and the countryside which it burns with its fiery breath is the second piece. Maybe the dragon is a perfect and complete thing that only doesn't fit in this world.

But when the dragon's teeth are sewn into the ground, humans spring up from them. Full humans, complete humans.

Isn't this hope? Isn't this the sign of another path?

It is a bloody and a difficult path. Each tooth must be torn from the flame-charred gums of the dragon, or rather, the rest of the dragon must be removed from the teeth, which is no different. This is also an ending in violence.

And yet, a monster can become something complete, something human. If the teeth of the dragon, the cruelest and most hateful part, can be transformed into people, with heads that fit their bodies, what can't I be transformed into?

It is foolish. It is impossible. There are a hundred reasons against it. But if it weren't possible, would I be writing this bestiary? If my prison is perfect, I want to understand its perfection, and if there is an escape...

The dragon is the monster of change, and change is the first name for hope.

PERSEUS

Perseus is not a monster.

Perseus is a human. Perseus arms himself with a sharp sword and a mirrored shield and goes forward to end in violence. There is no ending in violence without a Perseus to raise the sword and bring it down like a diving hawk.

Whatever must end in violence is a monster.

When I think of Perseus, of all the humans who arm themselves to kill, I think of the Cyclops. I think of something incomplete. I have called humans complete because they have a head and a body that fit each other, but even the Chimera would have a bloody hole if not for its lion head.

Humans are not complete. They may have one head and two eyes, but every human is born lacking. And when, like the Cyclops, they close off their lack, call themselves complete, then, they become monstrous.

They become Perseus.

What is the piece humans lack?

It is the world.

It is other humans.

It is all the other things that lack.

I could fit into the lack of a human. A hundred humans could fit into mine.

But if humans are monsters too, then what isn't?

Isn't there hope after all?

THE SATYR

The Satyr is part man and part goat. A goat lives among the difficult mountains and lost places of the world, while a human lives wherever it must live. A goat has horns to defend itself and a human has only its own cruelty. A goat is not a human, cannot be a human, and a human cannot be a goat, but the satyr is both and the satyr is joyful. He dances to the music of pipes in the forest, and even I cannot help but wish to dance with him when I hear his melody play.

The satyr ends in joy, not violence.

There is no such thing as a joyful monster.

The satyr is something else, a non-human, non-monster. There is something else, something else which is allowed, which plays music it is good to dance to. A goat's legs can top themselves with a human or a goat. It is a choice, and there is choice, and neither choice is wrong and maybe neither is right either. The human is and the satyr is and the human and the satyr are.

The satyr is not a monster. It is a joyful, loving thing, and joy is the second and secret name for hope.

TYPHON

Typhon is the God of monsters. He exists in legends whispered among monsters, which is to say everyone.

Every monster prays to Typhon, even if they don't know they pray.

Typhon is power. Typhon is hope.

Typhon stands a hundred feet tall and has a hundred heads, which is to say, endless heads and endless bodies. Typhon is everything that is incomplete brought together, everything that is monstrous made whole and given power.

Power is another name for hope.

Typhon is another name for hope, an impossible hope, a monster hope.

Let me build a hope that stands tall like Typhon, with a hundred heads each different from the last. Let my hope walk over the mountains and plain, tower over every structure that was built to dwarf hope, to dwarf those who were supposed to be without it. Let my hope have serpent fingers, and let its head touch the stars that hang over those who call it strange and frightening.

Let my hope end in anything other than violence.

Let my hope be powerful.

Let my hope be joy.

Let my hope be total.

Any hope that is not total is incomplete. Anything that is incomplete is a monster.

IN PRAISE OF NONVIOLENT TUESDAYS

/ Sal Kang

you should always

keep your daughters

on a leash

if there is love

there must also be

a non-love

/ / maybe this lineage has already translated itself into
my habits / I am afraid of anything unconditional /
violence is the bell & my heart is Pavlov's dog / I wait
for love like it is the answer / because his hands & lips
still know what I want & allow it / I learned this sound
from people who liked to remind me of their care by
punching a hole in the wall / by teaching their children
how to brace for impact / I know the face / the one
that folds like God's shadow / to keep them happy
I've been gone / / /

that comes with it

ruin

is a necessary side effect

let me know

when you figure this out

on your own

THE FINGER THAT ACHES

/ Sal Kang

when experiencing

stomach pains, prick

your finger with a needle

//

eyes half closed, I wait to feel

every joint of your finger

on my tongue

//

I wonder why they didn't nail Jesus's fingers

that'd hurt more

[

]

when leaving fingerprints

on glass, always

remember to wipe it clean

]

[

pinky promise, he said,

before the Christmas he stopped

visiting home

]

the boy stapled his finger like

he was trying to prove

painlessness

[
[
[

might as well point

at the dirt under my fingernails

& call it home

when leaving fingerprints

on men, consider them

dirtied forever

CRUSTACEANS & SKIN CELLS & OTHER THINGS THAT PEEL EASY

/ Sal Kang

another day goes by unattended

> another selection of women
> > another hour spent trying
> to look one in the eye

it's not my fault that her smile
makes me feel like a crab
sputtering in a pan of oil

> it's not that you look
> > particularly menacing it's just
> that lately i meet people
> > & study their fingernails first

lately i meet people & try
to calculate how fast they could
skin me

/

i'm told that they learn
about us in schools, *hikikomori*

> more shellfish than human
> more sun-scared than sick

but what they don't
teach you is what happens
when you get too attached
to a sanctuary that'll eventually
tighten around your body

what happens when you hear
a knock on the door &
start imagining the floorboards
crumbing from the sound
the news warns of my status
as financial burden

tells me   *try not to die*
inside since the odor will
suffocate those around you

i've gotten into the habit
of sleeping with the blinds rolled up

so someone knows to discover
my withering limbs
before they go too stale

every day i put rice
in my mouth & apologize
to the farmers that harvested it

every day i get up & try
to work & these four walls fold
over on top of each other

i'm sorry i'm sorry i'm sorry i'm sorry i'm sorry i'm sorry i'm
i'm sorry i'm sorry i'm sorry i'm sorry i'm sorry i'm sorry i'm
i'm sorry i'm sorry i'm sorry i'm sorry i'm sorry i'm sorry i'm
i'm sorry i'm sorry i'm sorry i'm sorry i'm sorry i'm sorry i'm
i'm sorry i'm sorry i'm sorry i'm sorry i'm sorry i'm sorry i'm
i'm sorry i'm sorry i'm sorry i'm sorry i'm sorry i'm sorry i'm

ESSAY ON NATURAL HISTORY

/ Coleman Edward Dues

Let's say that you have a rat in a box with a lever.[1] Muscles move into place like autonomous parts of a severed insect.[2] As death is the limit of human life in the realm of time, madness is its limit in animality, and just as death had been sanctified by the death of Christ, madness, in its most bestial nature, had also been sanctified.[3]

The parched plants of the desert fought for life, growing far apart, sending enormous roots deep to pierce the sand and split the rock for moisture, arming every leaf with a barbed thorn or poisoned sap, never thriving and ever thirsting.[4] But at the same time it was necessary to produce the geometrically straight lines, planes, circles, cylinders, cones, spheres, required in the detail of the machines.[5] Now on the landscape of the death earth, the Luftwaffe continues to fly into Volkswagens through the asphalt skies of death.[6]

It is supposed that a rifle and a penis are similar.[7] I am not unaware how shocking this word might seem here.[8] To deny this is to think that an object cannot be identical with itself, which is impossible (and so only true in an impossible world).[9] Anybody can tell this the minute they pick up any ordinary book any ordinary newspaper any ordinary advertisement or read any ordinary road sign or slang or conversation.[10] Hollywood itself tells us the background is composed of voices speaking from beyond their own annihilation.[11] Isn't it plain that sheets of moss, except that they have no tongues, could lecture all day if they wanted about spiritual patience?[12]

The insides of the machine at night like a garden of carnivorous plants.[13] We wanted to kill ourselves, but we also wanted to buy shoes, or become productive adults, and sometimes we aspired to innocence, to elder modes of personhood, but there was something antique, almost quaint about personhood, especially when this era of constant war was just sliding into view.[14] What we have left of Whitman's discredited dream of cultural revolution are paper ghosts and a sharp-eyed witty program of despair.[15] Out of the sea, the drive of oil, socket and grave, the brassy blood, flower, flower, all all and all.[16]

Let us consider a row of cherry trees.[17] Mother, monogamy, romance.[18] She entered the root of space through that immaterial window and disappeared.[19] Her eyelids flicker in the night.[20] Secretive persons tend to generalized memories, discreet editings, and the inevitable seasoning of sugar.[21] Tree conversations are still far above our heads.[22]

Legend has it that during WWI, soldiers of the Austrian Empire would order the Spritz to enliven and add depth to the local bubbly.[23] Instruments of war transformed into instruments of peace (from scales and armor, feathers and hair).[24] Had the ability to kill someone on the street walk back and finish a joke.[25] Yet he is neither here nor there because the mind moves everywhere; and he is neither now nor then because tomorrow comes again, foreshadowed, and the ragged wing of yesterday's remembering cuts sharply the immediate moon; nor is he always: late and soon becoming, never being, till becoming is a being still.[26] Sky a cadmium yellow from the fires to the north.[27]

A few white clouds all rushing eastward, a line of elms plunging and tossing like horses, and everyone, everyone, pointing up and shouting![28] They're coming, bringing their memory movies, some work to take with us to the moon, this long overdue blotch.[29] Rifts and sagas fill the air, and beautiful old women sing of them, so the air is filled with music and the smell of berries and apples and shouting when a gun goes off and crying in closed rooms.[30] Only above the U.S.A. city was the sky blank of stars; its color was pearly and blank.[31]

Agape, he observes the clouds and what is hanging in them: globes, penal codes, dead cats floating on their backs, locomotives.[32] He catalogues his past in terms of fashion and fads, public events and private fantasies, with such honesty and accuracy and in such abundance that, sooner or later, his history coincides with ours and we are hooked.[33] He glances upward, like he's looking for rain before stepping out from under an awning.[34] Reaching home mechanically, without taking off his uniform, he lay down on the sofa and...

died.[35] It has made his job easier, he noted, archly.[36] God could do without the ichthyosauri and the mastodon.[37]

In a word, is it not because the atoms were, at some remote epoch of time, even *more than together*—is it not because originally, and therefore normally, they were *One*—that now, in all circumstances—at all points—in all directions—by all modes of approach—in all relations and through all conditions—they struggle *back* to this absolutely, this irrelatively, this unconditionally one?[38] Every little piece was an individual animal with a built-in desire to protect its own life.[39] Is there even a boundary between you and the non-living world, or will the atoms in this page be a part of your body tomorrow?[40] Bestiality has a new status in this cycle of marriage exchange.[41]

Coming Soon, a new modern look to your bill.[42] Here it is again, like an appearing-disappearing monolith in the desert, ominous and numinous at the same time.[43]

One way to solve a hard problem is to think of a simpler but similar one, recall how you solved it, and then apply that technique to the harder problem.[44] Don't bring none of that silly shit to my gig, Moses said.[45] We hate the doctrine of utility, even in a philosopher, and much more in a poet; for the only real utility is that which leads to enjoyment, and in the end is, in all cases, better than the means.[46] There was a brief pause and when he spoke next his voice was soft and matter of fact.[47]

Meaning here slides away from a directed purpose into a perpetual overturning of signs that never coalesce into an exchangeable identity.[48] In silence and slow time, it was gradually resurrected and became a foster child later generations adopted with their various understandings of its nature.[49] Regardless of which interpretation one gives to probability, however, there is a consensus that the mathematics of probability are the same in either case.[50] Not for these the paper nautilus constructs her thin glass shell.[51]

Riverrun, past Eve and Adam's, from swerve of shore to bend of bay, brings us back by a commodious vicus of recirculation back to Howth Castle and Environs.[52] Outside the youth center, between the liquor store and the police station, a little dogwood tree is losing its mind; overflowing with blossomfoam, like a sudsy mug of beer; like a bride ripping off her clothes, dropping snow white petals to the ground in clouds, so Nature's wastefulness seems quietly obscene.[53] They also applauded her for showing her range, pole dancing in one scene and feeding an infant in the next.[54] The placid river and the green, lush mountains make the almost hour-long journey a lasting experience.[55] We accept her the way we accept ourselves, in blind ignorance, unable to put a name to the grief of existing.[56]

Notched into a cut of red clay crowned with oaks the road appeared to stop off short, like a cut ribbon.[57] In the south, grasslands turned a barren brown and harvests withered under the scorching sun; in the north, fires stalked forests and peat moss, the surfaces of rivers gleaming with dead floating salmon.[58] We can no longer afford to remain captives to the tendency of the more traditional sciences to dissect phenomena and examine their fragments.[59] Jesus wept.[60] Then dissolves in the rush toward the remote.[61]

No one ever knew there was coal in them mountains, till a man from the northeast arrived.[62] Behind them the line of woods gaped like a dark open mouth.[63] Senseless and purposeless were wood and iron and steam in their endless labours; but the persistence of their monotonous work was rivalled in tireless endurance by the strong crowds, who, with sense and with purpose, were busy and restless in seeking after—what?[64] A technological advance that appears not to threaten freedom often turns out to threaten it very seriously later on.[65] They carried the sky.[66]

A white parachute popped open suddenly in a surprising puff.[67] He arrived, a purpled creature, violet and squirming, face crushed into an emperor's expression.[68] These are the stories of those extraordinary American Airmen who have gone above and beyond to accomplish what many once thought was impossible.[69] You've been killed, don't you remember?[70] The demonstration comes to an end with a flourish.[71] The machine runs silent for a moment.[72] That's about all that can be said for plots, which anyway are just one thing after another, a what and a what and a what.[73]

But all these things did not come together.[74] The dance-hall music changes to a tango that has a minor and somewhat ominous tone.[75] Beside the piano the Christmas tree now stands stripped of ornament, burned-down candle stubs on its ragged branches.[76] Soon bad things start to happen—one by one the girls disappear and there's lots and lots of very, very unrealistic blood, body parts and mayhem.[77] According to eyewitness reports offered after the event, several old men were bayoneted, praying women and children were shot in the back of the head, and at least one girl was raped and then killed.[78] I lit a cigarette to distance myself from this statement.[79] Maintaining a media focus on slow violence poses acute challenges, not only because it is spectacle deficient, but because the fallout's impact may range from the cellular to the transnational and (depending on the specific character of the chemical or radiological hazard) may stretch beyond the horizon of imaginable time.[80] The trail of the human serpent is thus over everything.[81]

Look down at your body and whisper *there is no home like you.*[82] A country that is bruised but whole, benevolent but bold, fierce and free.[83] He took his wife to a remote African island to negotiate with the tribe elders, including 3 priests, the sacred method to gain 6 inches on his manhood.[84] They're fond of arrows dipped in a neurotoxin that will stop your heart in one minute—and they have bones reinforced with naturally-occurring carbon fiber.[85] All this does not sound very ill, and the last was not at all amiss, for they wear no breeches.[86] The land flourished because it was fed from so many sources—because it was nourished by so many cultures and traditions and peoples.[87] Let's take a closer look at that birth certificate.[88]

While the system works well enough for most transactions, it still suffers from the inherent weaknesses of the trust based model.[89] If you can imagine a toadstool in joints, an interminable string of toadstools, budding and sprouting in endless convolutions—why, that is something like it.[90] To seduce a fact into becoming an object, a pleasing one, with some kind of esthetic quality, which would also add to the store of knowledge and even extend through several strata of history, like a pin through a cracked wrist bone, connecting these in such a dynamic way that one would be forced to acknowledge a new kind of superiority without which the world could no longer conduct its business, even simple stuff like bringing water home from wells, coal to hearths, would of course be an optimal form of it but in any case the thing's got to come into being, something has to happen, or all we'll have left is disagreements, *désagréments*, to name a few.[91] Everybody in America is angry about something.[92] Thus it could be conceived of as an adulterated fragment of the surrounding cosmic fire, and so as the possessor in some degree of that fire's directive power.[93] Hurtling across the sky, a missile has mistaken a vehicle for a helicopter, exploding in a ball of white flame.[94]

Or in the end, is there not also to be found in our own endeavor, if in general we need to compare it, a concealed evading in the face of something which we—and indeed not by accident—no longer see?[95] Everything we call real is made of things that cannot be regarded as real.[96] Hail nothing full of nothing, nothing is with thee.[97]

This world in arms is not spending money alone.[98] They call it easing the Spring: if you have any strength in your thumb: like the bolt, and the breech, and the cocking-piece, and the point of balance, which in our case we have not got; and the almond blossom silent in all of the gardens and the bees going backwards and forwards, for today we have naming of parts.[99] To define is to kill.[100] The result is a global linguistic machine that offers templates not only for words but also for thoughts; that values information over affect; and that reinforces the long history of the alphabet's dominance over Western thinking.[101]

Daddy won't sell the farm.[102] Time's going has ebbed the moorings to the memories that make this city-kid part farm-boy.[103] Beneath the threadbare trinomial accounting of acres, bales, and hands, some discerned a deeper economy.[104] The hundred-thousandth lyric published this decade in which a plainspoken persona realizes a small profundity about suburban bourgeois life, or the hundred-thousandth coming-of-age novel developing psychological portraits of characters amid difficult romantic relationships and family tensions, is somehow still within the bounds of the properly creative (and those numbers are not exaggerations); yet the first or second work to use previously written source texts in a novel way are still felt to be troublingly improper.[105] That's no more serious than if he said he's going to drop a bomb on the Vatican.[106]

It's true for bees as it is for human beings: life brings sickness with it.[107] It remains to be added that the organism is resolved to die only in its own way; even these watchmen of life were originally the myrmidons of death.[108] But no personality test, or series of tests, will ever replace the depth and fullness of the perception of self which can be achieved when the mind alters its state of consciousness sufficiently to perceive the very hologram of itself which it has projected into the universe in its proper context as a part of the universal hologram in a totally holistic and intuitional way.[109] Damn, what am I saying?[110]

We already committed murder, we might as well rob his ass![111] Each part is a blossom under his touch to which the fibres of her being stem one by one, each to its end, until the whole field is a white desire, empty, a single stem, a cluster, flower by flower, a pious wish to whiteness gone over—or nothing.[112] The sexual act is in time what the tiger is in space.[113] Orchids are gushing out from the faucets.[114] There's only five colors this time, but they're no less of an irritation.[115] O night, you take the petals of the roses in your hand, but leave the stark core of the rose to perish on the branch.[116]

The last image was too immediate for any eye to register.[117] That big crazyman was really the kiss of death.[118] Rarely does a man die without having a few more folds to undo.[119] The crystal was gone but it ticked.[120] Then off the eye flies to the whiteness verge upon verge.[121]

For, they were themselves, these actors—these people were themselves.[122] You misinterpret everything, even the silence.[123] I just need you to recognize that this shit is killing you, too, however much more softly, you stupid motherfucker, you know?[124]

In time, submarine seamounts, or islands, are formed.[125] Our mother of puddled images fading away into deep blue polymer.[126] Temperatures are just above freezing, and everything is drowning in darkness.[127] Someday, I swear, we're gonna go to a place where we can do everything we want to, and we can pet the crocodiles.[128]

WORKS CITED

1. Paul T. Mason, Randi Kreger, *Stop Walking on Eggshells*

2. William Burroughs, *Naked Lunch*

3. Michel Foucault, *Madness and Civilization: A History of Insanity in the Age of Reason*

4. Zane Grey, *The Heritage of the Desert*

5. Karl Marx, *Capital: A Critique of Political Economy*

6. Bob Kaufman, "The Ancient Rain," *The Ancient Rain: Poems 1956-1978*

7. Wilfred Bion, *Attention and Interpretation*

8. Jacques Derrida, "Différance," *Margins of Philosophy*

9. Paul Kabay, *On the Plenitude of Truth: A Defense of Trivialism*

10. Gertrude Stein, "Lecture One," *Lectures in America*

11. Rae Armantrout, "Again," *Next Life*

12. Mary Oliver, "Landscape," *Dream Work*

13. Charles Simic, "The Big Machine," *The Book of Gods and Devils*

14. Ariana Reines, foreword to *Zirconia*.........*Bad Bad,* by Chelsea Minnis

15. Susan Sontag, introduction to *On Photography*

16. Dylan Thomas, "All All and All the Dry World's Lever," *The Collected Poems of Dylan Thomas, 1934-52*

17. Ernest Fenollosa, *The Chinese Written Character as a Medium for Poetry*

18. Aldous Huxley, *Brave New World*

19. Alejandro Jodorowsky, *Albina and the Dog-Men*

20. Eimear McBride, *A Girl Is a Half-Formed Thing*

21. Elizabeth Hardwick, *Sleepless Nights*

22. Robin Wall Kimmerer, *Braiding Sweetgrass*

23. The back of a bottle of Cappelletti Aperitvo

24. Friedrich Nietzsche, *The Will to Power*

25. Michael Ondaatje, *The Collected Works of Billy the Kid*

26. Stanley Kunitz, "Change," *Selected Poems, 1928-1958*

51. Marianne Moore, "The Paper Nautilus," *The Complete Poems of Marianne Moore*

52. James Joyce, *Finnegans Wake*

53. Tony Hoagland, "A Color of the Sky," *What Narcissism Means to Me*

54. Erica Gonzales, "Cardi B Breastfeeds in Her Insanely Epic 'Money' Music Video," *Harper's Bazaar*

55. The liner notes to *Sailing Along the Wailua River,* by Captain Walter Smith Sr.

56. Nathalie Léger, *Suite for Barbara Loden*

57. William Faulkner, *The Sound and the Fury*

58. Andreas Malm, *Fossil Capital: The Rise of Steam Power and the Roots of Global Warming*

59. Murray Bookchin, *The Ecology of Freedom: The Emergence and Dissolution of Hierarchy*

60. *The King James Bible*

61. Rosmarie Waldrop, *Reluctant Gravities*

62. Darrell Scott, "You'll Never Leave Harlan Alive," *Aloha from Nashville*

63. Flannery O'Connor, "A Good Man Is Hard to Find"

64. Elizabeth Gaskell, *North and South*

65. Ted Kaczynski, *Industrial Society and Its Future*

66. Tim O'Brien, *The Things They Carried*

67. Joseph Heller, *Catch-22*

68. Tina Chang, "Revolutionary Kiss," *Hybrida*

69. U.S. Air Force Recruitment Website

70. Adrian Lyne, *Jacob's Ladder*

71. Athol Fugard, *"Master Harold"…and the Boys*

72. Arthur Miller, *Death of a Salesman*

73. Margaret Atwood, "Happy Endings"

74. Joyce Carol Oates, "Where Are You Going, Where Have You Been?"

75. Tennessee Williams, *The Glass Menagerie*

76. Henrik Ibsen, *A Doll House*

77. Three-star IMDb review of Japanese horror film *House*

78. PBS, "The Mai Lai Massacre"

79. Ben Lerner, *Leaving the Atocha Station*

80. Rob Nixon, *Slow Violence and the Environmentalism of the Poor*

81. William James, "What Pragmatism Means," *Essays in Pragmatism*

82. Rupi Kaur, "thank you," *Milk and Honey*

83. Amanda Gorman, "The Hill We Climb," *The Hill We Climb and Other Poems*

84. Spam email

85. James Cameron, *Avatar*

86. Michel de Montaigne, "Of Cannibals," *Essays*

87. Lyndon B. Johnson

88. Tweet by Donald J. Trump

89. Satoshi Nakamoto, "Bitcoin: A Peer-to-Peer Electronic Cash System"

90. Charlotte Perkins Gilman, "The Yellow Wallpaper"

91. John Ashberry, "One Coat of Paint," *April Galleons*

92. Anthony Braxton

93. G.S Kirk, J.E. Raven, and M. Schofield, *The Presocratic Philosophers*

94. Henri Cole, "War Rug," *Poem-a-Day*

95. Martin Heidegger, *Kant and the Problem of Metaphysics*

96. Neils Bohr

97. Ernest Hemingway, "A Clean, Well-Lighted Place"

98. Dwight D. Eisenhower, the Chance for Peace Speech

99. Henry Reed, "Naming of Parts," *Henry Reed: Collected Poems*

100. Stéphane Mallarmé

101. Peter Schwenger, *Asemic: The Art of Writing*

102. Montgomery Gentry, "Daddy Won't Sell the Farm," *Tattoos and Scars*

103. Geffrey Davis, "What I Mean When I Say Farmhouse," *Revising the Storm*

104. Walter Johnson, *River of Dark Dreams*

FIG. 13

/ Callie Ingram

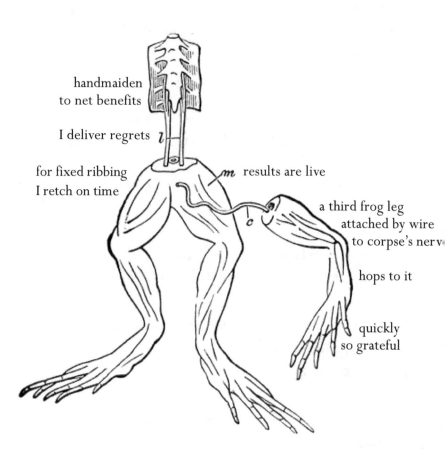

handmaiden
to net benefits

I deliver regrets

for fixed ribbing
I retch on time

results are live

a third frog leg
attached by wire
to corpse's nerve

hops to it

quickly
so grateful

l {
god a spinal cord – worked upon
nodding out a rhythm of exposure
patched voice without story
– unless pulse carries – I am
because I deliver / I am
delivering / delivered / de-livered
livered / liver / live –
my great works clench, cast – –

m {
– – prick, pray pay
– pulled ache
pared, a breath too
bare / I carry
– I carry – I carry – –

c {
– – my own? scavenge passive
for my purposes / I did not ask
to tremble, follow – magic body
mirror, who is the furthest? I do
gorge, I cannot help / living
to burn off the fuel of others'
fluids / carcass eating carcass
– I jump faster & just the same

NEURASTHENOTAXONOMIA

/ Callie Ingram

the neurasthenic
the hysterical
subject the
hypochondriacal
the neurasthenics
the subject under
discussion
the patient the
neurasthenic the
next victim

the atmosphere
the approach of a
storm the clouds
the presentiment of
a storm

the most
significant features
the time the pitch
the sound of a loud
noise the crash

the remark the
complaint the habit
of swearing the
course of his
soliloquies the
meaning of the
word

the region of the
spine the minds of
many people the
nervous system the
phenomena the
picture the human
system

the matter with him
the latter condition
the result of a chill
the result of some
impairment the
usual result the
result

the housewife the
the workman the
commercial man
the parson
the pulpit the
society of his
children the street
the road the others
the man the woman

the future the
thought of it
the form of a fear
the unknown
the future

the patience to
listen the
opportunity of
calling the medical
aid the joy and zest
of life

the common lot of
mankind the
common cares of
life the power of
leaving the
hours of recreation
the lightest
literature the
slightest reason

the tiredness the
gentle aching the
weariness the
languor the solace
of amusing
themselves
the greatest
pleasure the
solitude of their
own thoughts
the nervous tension
the worst dread the
fear

the very opposite
the very disaster
the same the down
grade the worse
things get the top
of everything else
the inevitable
climax the most
preventable of
conditions

the harder to locate
the harder they try
the critical
moments the effort
the different ways

the hours of work
the work the day
the morning the
work of the
following day the
work the evenings
the events of the
day the work of the
morrow the home
the work the
workhouse
the home

the signs the
symptoms the
verge of a
breakdown the
various signs of
neurasthenia or
breakdown the
most constant
symptoms the
worst symptom of
all the first signs of
this malady the
clearest danger
signal the first sign
the first the
premonitory signs
the preliminary
stages

THE FAMILY PHOTO ALBUMS

/ Day Heisinger-Nixon

[image description: ███'s father before he was one, his face still smooth and featureless.]

[image description: ███, approximately nine years old, crowned with a pair of paper rabbit ears. Oleander, rose-warm and rippling, creeps up along the fence behind them. (Not shown: their pink lungs contracting, contracting, contracting, and blooming open).]

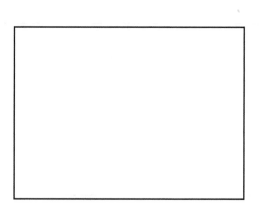

[image description: ███'s mother with a child in her arms, July in her eyes (and tears, and everything else).]

[image description:

KAISER
PERMANENTE ®

09-25-2019

RX:

▮▮▮▮, ▮▮▮▮▮

Mf: AUROBINDO PHARM

sertraline 25 mg tablet
GENERIC FOR: Zoloft

Take 3 tablets by mouth daily at bedtime

green, film-coated, scored, oblong, tablet, A, 1 6

Claim RX: ▮▮▮▮▮

Discard: 09/25/2020

Btl 1 of 1 QTY: 300/300

Refills 0

LL

 ]

[image description: A snippet from a duration of time, full of the things time tends to be filled with (sun, teeth, movement, shades of blue, babies), everyone reacting accordingly.]

[image description: ▮▮▮▮ and ▮▮▮▮, two displaced children, attempting to squeeze themselves into a thin American
weather.]

[image description: A stretch of road so busy with human life that it negates any other type. Beetles bursting fat and blue on slick windshields. Monarchs being swept up into grills with gaping mouths. Carcasses of small and no longer identifiable animals draping themselves along the shoulders of the road like fur scarves. A stretch of road like any other site from a whole class of human-life-sustaining-death-producing places littered with movement, static, and sound, rubbed raw of life. (Other possible interpretations: a mall, a bus terminal, a subway station in Santiago or DC, a construction site, an airport in Berlin, an airport in Istanbul, an airport in Montevideo, an airport in Fresno, a hospital or a bed inside it.)]

[image description: Form in the lack thereof. (A body, then none at all.)]

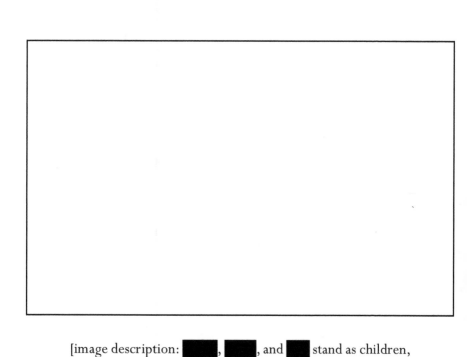

[image description: ████, ████, and ███ stand as children, side-by-side, sweaty, smiling. Behind them, the last summer presses its shoulder into the horizon.]

CLINICAL FILE, GENETICS: ASSESSMENT AND DIAGNOSIS
/ Day Heisinger-Nixon

Do any immediate family members exhibit signs of greater than average joint laxity or skin hyperextensibility, fragility, or bruising?

HZHDolls ★ ★ ★ ★ ★ (130)

Rescued Liv Doll - Fully Articulated, Jointed, Pose-able Doll, Blond Hair with Pink Stra

$17.00　　　　　Message Sell

Free shipping to United States

Add to cart

Like advertised, the body is fully articulated. It bends at the joints and is articulate. The dictionary is full of words I would never use for home, but, once, when I was a child, an uncle of mine left a voicemail and then fully (dis)articulated. I convinced myself afterwards it was his head in the urn: a chia pet pop-top we could pour water into to bring him back to life. Once, in a Bolivian cemetery, I glanced into an adobe structure and saw burnt plastic and human femurs and skulls. When I asked if it was a crematorium, the groundskeeper told me it wasn't. He told me it was for trash.

Is there any familial history of heart attack, organ prolapse, aneurysm, or sudden death?

In Soviet-controlled Eastern Europe, the pipe organ was a banned instrument. Too much god in the brass. Too many kings. All my keys are made of teeth and bone. All my teeth, made of cherrywood. The past is a foreign country, and things are done differently there. The church chatters even in the best of us. This is what it means to grow up inside of a red verb. The country— the red verb.

Apply the Beighton Scale to test for general range of motion and joint hypermobility. What is your cumulative score?

With Rothko and Martin, the trick is to look past the painting. To catch the field. We all greet the morning grass at least a few times in our lives. *¡Buen día, pastito!* Galeano writes, recording the child in his midst. What comes next, here and often, is the score you were asking about. Music, you might say.

Do you experience any darkening, starry, or haloed vision, fainting or near-fainting, or sudden rise or fall in heart rate, particularly after changing positions?

When the burning celestial body slid through the clouds above Tuolumne Meadows, spinning from one lip of the valley to the other, even our Starry Night guide was caught off guard. *I have no idea,* he said, *I've never seen anything like it.* It was too large and too constant to be a meteor or a shooting star. An angel, someone suggested. *Look, there's her halo. Right there.* The rapture, offered another. China's disarticulated Long March 7 rocket, we would learn, a week later. We were right. Or at least some of us were.

Have you experienced any musculoskeletal pain in excess of three months? If so, where?

The body of a beef cow can be divided into the ribs, the short loin, the brisket, the flank, and so on. At the animal sanctuary in Acton there's a steer who once had his intestines torn out by coyotes. The farmer handling him shoved them back inside his belly and sutured him up with duct tape. Now, the steer squints in the sun. Now, I pray he remembers only a life in which he was never a sacrifice to the god of small efficiencies. Each month that my darlings and I stay alive and full of most of our own organs is another month we avoid a dirt-based kind of intimacy. What I mean to say is: it all hurts, every single muscle.

Describe any dislocations, subluxations, and frank joint instability that you have experienced.

My grandmother tells the story of their dislocation best: that two hundred years before the cobalt sheet of nocturnal self-exile, her ancestors and mine were led to the River Volga by promises of free soil and sweet corn. And when they arrived: Camels! Camels in the tundra, their callused rubber knees knocking in the snow. Their wool, fashioned into one coat after another. In the haze of these things, everyone would forget to tell the story of the dislocation *of the camels*. Of what led *them* to that land of little sun. Of how little corn had to do with any of it.

Based on your physical exam and history, you have been assigned a clinical diagnosis of Hypermobile Ehlers-Danlos Syndrome, a genetic connective tissue disorder caused by the production of faulty collagen. While hEDS primarily affects the joints, skin, and blood-vessel walls, it is associated with a wide variety of other complications. Before leaving today, please note anything else you would like to communicate with your healthcare provider below.

col•la•gen
/ˈkɑləgən/

> *noun*
> From the Greek κόλλα (kólla) "glue" + -γενής (-genḗs)"-forming," referring to the compound's early use in the process of boiling the skin and tendons of horses and other animals to obtain glue.

1 the main structural protein in the extracellular matrix of the various connective tissues of the body **2** as a schoolchild, I would tack the tips of my fingers together with nail glue for its subsequent shock **3** only back home would I rip them apart, my glueparts cracking and raw at first breath **4** my lungs clapping raw at first breath, burning mares galloping in the fumes **5** there is no scarcity of toxins, blistering skin among them **6** a well-made papier-mâché horse shudders off every fly that gets trapped in her glue **7** the clay in her hips cracks under every bone-borne storm

THE CATALYTIC CONVERTER AND THE DRY VEGETATION

/ Colette Arrand

I dream of cars set ablaze
my millions of blades
of dead grass—one last
protest, one last *what the fuck
are you doing here?* before
it all turns to smoke.
If I burn it will be because
I didn't reuse the tinfoil
the last time I made pizza rolls,
because I didn't separate
the bottlecap from its bottle,
because a book with my name
on it went to the landfill
and not a Little Free Library.
This moment of personal accountability
brought to you by ExxonMobile,
by Shell, by BP, by every balding man
in a suit with a name like Rex
who has chosen wealth over the future.
So many shows I watch are concerned
with the future that it's tempting
to say that I'm living for it, but nobody
there will remember my hat-chosen name.
All of the other names in that hat
have long since been discarded,
so apologies to Virginia Arrand
and Lily Arrand and Lindsay Arrand
and a dozen others I've fated to come down
with me to this literally scorched Earth,
and all the names I've forgotten. I asked
my psychiatrist why so many of my poems
involve me burning and stopped her mid
thought to say *Hitchcock was right*

about the bomb under the table,
only it's a gender reveal stunt or a car
left idling on dry grass. In truth
this never happened; it's a lie
meant to obfuscate how often I have to talk
about suicide, how often it feels
like I'm both the grass and the idling car.
It's hard to clean your tinfoil in this state,
when you're so far from Earth
all you can see is its potential to smolder.

THE FUTURE IS HERE AND EVERYTHING MUST BE DESTROYED

/ Colette Arrand

I think about the joke that circulates
on Twitter when the south gets battered
by weather, you know the one,
about how you know things
are *really* bad when the Waffle House
closes? On my way to Jacksonville
I am sitting in a Waffle House
because weather is battering the south.
Water is pouring into the place,
onto the floor, onto the jukebox,
into a bucket that splashes onto me
occasionally though I don't notice—
I am immolating and haven't yet realized
that, either. I am listening to the manager
talk shit about how she hopes the building
falls, everyone inside dead as a doornail
like one big fuck you to a corporation
that won't pay to fix the fucking roof.

I am with her in wishing I was dead.

I think the thing about that joke
is that it's meant as a compliment:
look at how proud these people are.
I think the thing about pride
is that what most people are reading
is what happens when a person
is trapped by the expectations
of capital. A person mans the griddle
during a storm because they'll be fired
otherwise, not as a testament
to the strength of the human spirit—
that any of us endure under capitalism

should be proof enough. I hope
this building *does* crumble. I hope I'm here
when it does. Since an apocalypse
isn't shit without flowers, I'll bring them.
They can be buried along with me.

SALT VAMPIRE

/ Colette Arrand

I.

It's Pride and I'm drinking
Diet Coke because Diet Coke advertises
during the Tonys and I'm sober
and can't drink the other sponsors

(Pride would like to thank
Skyy Vodka,
Barefoot Wine,
Bud Light
Heineken
Smirnoff
Captain Morgan
Don Julio
and Pabst Blue Ribbon
for their support)

no matter how much I'd like to. (and i'd always like to)

II.

While drinking Diet Coke
I wonder how badly discolored
my piss would look
to someone drinking it
were anyone here
to drink my piss.

III.

It's fucked how
the human body needs

water to survive, how
the alarm that sounds
when one is dehydrated
are headaches that feel
just like the headaches
I have every day

It's fucked how everybody
knows Diet Coke isn't water,
which didn't stop Diet Coke
from claiming it was water
during one of those Tonys campaigns

IV.

I drink Diet Coke
and my tongue
has the texture
of a pumice stone

I drink Diet Coke
and my lips,
when pressed
to a man's flesh,
feels like salted pavement;
the man's organ
a motorist
upset to be stuck
behind the salt truck

V.

Once, a man i did not kiss
told me that Diet Coke
would give me cancer
before offering me
his vape pen.

Is it weird

that I find comfort
in this potential?

VI.

When I drink Diet Coke
I imagine the aspartame
collecting in an organ
like poison in a water balloon,
a thing meant to burst,
meant to keep
the child wielding it
in suspense
until it does

This is how I see my body,
bloated and fragile
in the arms
of a clumsy lover,
ready to break.

Soak me in water
all you like;
what I fill my body with
will seep through my pores,
but I'll never stop being thirsty

THE AMERICAN RECONQUEST

/ Cajetan Sorich

It's a swamp. There's lots of carbon. That's the big thing. She knew this, and this was why she chose the swamp. Plus, Florida. It never gets cold. Her skin wouldn't crack, she'd meet new people, smell new plants. And, oh, does she smell new plants. Their burps. And alligator feces, and small, decomposing, fuzzy animals curled beneath the bubbling skin of the water.

Everything here is unfamiliar.

One of the few things she misses about the city is lines of striped traffic barricades, easel ones with the round, blinking lights on top. In the wet dark of the swamp she remembers how they looked when off duty, roped together, blinking in the icy dark like flickering lollipops. Sheer, hard, orange, all lined up like that.

In Chicago she would sometimes lean back in her work chair with her arms out, the chair back short enough for her shoulder blades to spread apart while free from the touch of anything but the air. She pretended that she was floating on her back in the sky. That was only at first and about as fun as things got overall.

Perhaps I'm exaggerating, but that's how I felt by the end, anyway. It seemed to me that everybody back there in the city was deeply unhappy. Then it burnt to a crisp on an unspecial morning. Or, again, so it felt.

You know how that goes. Over and over. And over. Someone out there, alone, in the dark, manages to find what looks, for a moment, like safety or peace, or even just a place to rest. And very soon the ugly forces that have been dogging this place since Europeans first arrived here show up, take it back, monetize it, and kick out whoever discovered it. That's a history as old as the Americas themself. Since, at least, they've been called the Americas.

With dew on my skin I decided it was time to try and sleep. I pressed the mushy button on the little blue radio and killed the broadcast.[1]

◆

At the top of my final year in Chicago I moved to a new apartment. It was summertime, and I found myself in a loft that at night became dank with cold river mist bouncing up from below. On even the muggiest summer nights I left the air off, for by dusk the mist took a vibrant scent and cooled my skin just enough. I would wake up every night at 3 a.m., wrapped in sheets slightly wet.

In the fall I maintained my ways. I did not turn on the heat at night. I did not want it to filter the river droplets back outside, or to obliterate them right there with its hot, dry breath.

Months later, near the end of October, I woke up at 3 a.m. covered in dew. I was cold, teeth chattering and knees knocking, a whole show. In only cotton undies and a wide silk shirt handed down to me from my grandmother, I vibrated over to my dresser for leggings. I slid a quivering leg into each pant. The dresser with its honey wood was pale blue under the moonlight pouring through eight foot windows. I had a nice place.

Framed by the fat glowing bulbs of the bathroom mirror my lips were pale blue. That wet cold had me wide awake. I ran a hot shower. I set a heavy fleece sweatshirt, two pairs of socks, and long underwear on the toilet, prepared to seal the shower heat into my body before the cold air could take it.

Most importantly, I would not turn on that sickening, dry heat.

Above the drawbridges of the Chicago River should not be a place for rogue living. There was no way my scrawny body was going to survive the coming fall nights without hypothermia.

Yet the thought of that fake air pumping through, a dry throat. I worked over forty hours each week to afford this soggy loft apartment at the top of a creaking millhouse, and I would keep it soggy.

That was the one part of my life I felt was still mine. The air inside my home. It was 5 a.m., and I still lay awake too cold.

I put on a teensy fisherman beanie that a whiny man I had slept

---

1   Michael S. Judge, *Death Is Just Around the Corner*, episode 67, "Thomas Pynchon and the American Reconquista, pt. 1"

with last week left behind and thin knit gloves, then transversed diagonally from my bed to the large open kitchen. I ground coffee beans and scooped them into the percolator. Standing in a spot where the shining wood floor has dulled slightly matte, I inhaled the smell of coffee mixing with crisp river air. The Bialetti gurgled over tiny blue flames, nearly echoing off of the obsidian countertops.

I had a vintage blue velour chair with a square wood frame, the same honey colored wood as my dresser and the beams that cut across the loft, which I curled in to sip my coffee. Two hours later, I watched one of the bridges dislodge and begin to rise.

✦

I hadn't yet fallen back asleep but my alarm rang. I had to get ready for work. I would think about my wet apartment later.

My head ached and I saw little white worms ping in the corners of my vision. Work was a fifteen minute walk. A law office, I was a legal assistant, mostly faxing and copying, but I was originally hired as a proofreader. My title had since expanded to assistantship to be more menial, but with more pay.

In the elevator I came to terms with how sleep deprived I was, how it was going to be a terrible day. At my stout oak desk I began to come to terms with the fact that I'd have to turn on the heat later. It was not plausible to trade sleep for moist river air. Allowing myself to be kept up by the cold was dysfunctional. I could not afford to be dysfunctional.

I got home at 8:30 that evening. Upon activating the heat, I realized I could not afford to live that way, either. I was suffocating. Merely five minutes in, I was suffocating.

After work I had gone to a sports bar under the L where I ate peanuts and drank vodka which turned red and blue against the flatscreens lining the walls. I would prepare carefully, I told myself. It would be fine. It was just a matter of becoming properly relaxed beforehand.

I asked for extra ice in my second vodka. They had large and serious square cubes that frosted the glass instantly.

It wasn't my usual routine to stop for an after work drink, even though my days at the firm sometimes stretched into ten hours. It wasn't my usual type of guy to approach me as I finished the second vodka, and it wasn't usual for me to say yes to a third.

He was a construction worker, or a dock guy of some sort. I don't remember. He had strayed to me from a table of men in the same blunt and dusty boots as his. We sat beside each other at the bar. In the cool light his nose cast an oblong shadow across his cheek.

He asked if I worked nearby and I said no. He asked if I lived nearby, and I especially said no. I was embarrassed by the prime location of my loft.

"I live in Beverly. Was in the city for a bit till Da died, just a bit ago, and now I got his house to look after."

"You have to?"

They had the TV in the corner blaring something political, or maybe just geographical. *The Congo, Iraq, Venezuela, Bolivia, South Vietnam, 1973 Chile*—Things started to blur, my chest warm.

"Well, it was his Da's before that."

His name was Artan. He had a crooked smile where the right side didn't rise as high as the left. I spent some time wondering what it reminded me of, until I realized it was of my own. Five root canals and fifteen cavities left some of my nerves dead, though I didn't know what his story was. His hair wasn't a warm red with orange undertones but a cool red with blue beneath. He had it cut short but long enough so he had some forehead tendrils. A little style, but not stylish enough so that he reminded me of the whiny metrosexual with the tiny hat.

I didn't share much about myself, but the more I looked at him the more I realized: a warm body was exactly what I needed that night.

Unfortunately, I threw up in my lap upon the fourth vodka.

Embarrassed but unable to balance on my own, I let him hail me a cab. I took it virtually around the corner. A waste. But I told Artan I didn't live nearby. I didn't want him to know I was a liar.

I waited to take off my coat until I was in my warm, steaming bathroom. I peeled off my puke soaked wool dress and opaque black tights. The hot water would surely infuse me with enough heat to make it through the night. Just one more. I would put it off as long as I could.

But I was not warm enough. I layered up, but the wetness in the air penetrated the duvet, my long underwear, in a way that normal cold could not. I became so desperate for just one more heatless night, that I called Artan afterall. I would tell him I was housesitting.

"Hello?"

"Hey," I said. "I'm feeling better. I'm sorry about that."

"About what?" I assumed he was trying to make light of my disgrace with a little joke. I laughed.

"Anyway, I was hoping you could come by. I know it's late, but it gets chilly up here." I was still drunk.

"What a nice surprise." He paused. "Certainly. I'll be there."

"Okay. Let me know when you're ready for the address."

"No need." Did I give it to him at the bar? Was I that drunk that I don't recall? Did I reveal my lie without even remembering?

I sat in my blue chair waiting for him. My phone rang but it wasn't Artan. It was the whiny man from last week.

Oh, Jesus. That explained the address thing. It was not Artan who I'd called.

I did not answer. In blue despair, I turned on that life sucking heat.

✦

This was not the real tragedy of it all, of living in Chicago, of skin being stripped by artifical hot air. Because the real tragedy was the fat black market government subsidized bullets that could penetrate bricks, cement, cedar shingle siding, wood clapboard siding, fiber cement home siding, vinyl and aluminum siding, and even seamless steel siding; especially great for busting through peasants, communists, working class, Triangle Shirtwaisters, revolutionaries, Sandinistas, Black Panthers, Kennedy Brothers, artists, any genuine counterculture. Holes right through uprisings, through nationalization of oil, of rising literacy and lowering poverty rates.

This is why she chose the swamp. It's outside. What good are walls in this day and age? What good is any space she has carved from a whirring hell for her solace? Even her childhood home was uprooted in the 2008 crisis. As long as her lifespan overlaps with the Highway of Death and combing Bolivia for lithium, she will try to stay outside. Outside, the air is just the air.

Unless it's the insurmountably bitter cold Chicago winter air.

She reduces her belongings to one fat suitcase. As she packs she listens to college radio through her little blue speaker.

◆

A swamp, aside from the carbon, is simply low ground that collects water. It is wet, forested land. There are true swamps and transitional swamps, which are swamps that are too wet to grow trees but too shallow to be marshes. A marsh is a swamp with no trees. A true swamp has trees. They are flooded forests.

She is in a true swamp. In the dark she falls asleep staring at a sky blacker than she's ever seen. Her ceiling is layers of stars and the ghoulish silhouettes of standing trees and fallen trees and twisted trees.

◆

In the mornings there are green vines and thick, sexy ferns. Very sexy ferns. I live for the ferns, now.

Before I got the walking distance law job, I would sip hot coffee every morning at the bus stop, overcoming the chill with thick brown steam rising from my thermos. That was when I first moved. Now, during my mornings in this subsequent new beginning, I look at the ferns.

It was an easy journey. The worst part was losing my headphones at the airport. The plane to Florida was all engine. But when I landed I already noticed I was different.

My brain doesn't cycle over imaginary checklists like it used to. Now it's concrete, the way one's earliest memories often are. Primordial. Sounds and shapes smudging into bright white auras.

There were engine sounds then soft ferns and then my pure, wet toes nubbing into mud and a sky uninhibited by rooftop shingles or paper-thin vinyl siding. Then, as night deepened, there were only ironworks and cadences.

I wondered: Where do I sleep?

Plastic is so light that it floats on the dark swamp water. It is so light that I can sleep right on the water, floating on a plastic tarp.

◆

There is a phenomenon here where organic gas bubbles sometimes combust across the top of the water. They scared me at first. Tiny bonfires spark in my periphery as soft waves from stirring alligators rock me to sleep.

I wake up in the middle of the night. Tiny combustions against silky onyx mirror the stars in the sky. I cannot differentiate the two, and it is like I'm floating in space.

The next blare that wakes me is sunlight.

I've begun a routine.

I slosh over the five inches of water that coat my floating tarp walkway. Under the trees at the edge of the water, I velcro my sandals. Strappy sporty little guys, the only pair I brought with. I store them in the open belly of my bedside log.

I walk fifteen minutes to the bus and wait. As I dressed earlier the sun was bright yet cool, but now it's hot light. The temperature in Florida does that. It rises aggressively by the minute. I want this.

I didn't always know it, but I've never been able to live without gas flames bursting in my peripheral, never without a mean sun. Never without sloshing through wetlands with their ever-changing levels. Never without dank swampy fog rising from the cement.

It's no mind now. Here I am, where I've always wanted to be, with the prehistoric mosquitoes. I am removed from all options in both blank and already formed spaces. Finally, it's okay to rest.

I will no longer be able to stand in the cold and stare at the traffic easels roped into rows of twinkling lollipops, but the wind will not burn my eyes.

I will no longer be able to stare out of brilliant floor to ceiling loft windows, but I don't need them anymore because I'm already outside.

I couldn't walk around barefoot like I can here. I tried from time to time, my feet stuck by the corners of milky salt crystals, white spots of irritation blooming across them; the skin between my toes so dry. Brittle, really. It cracked, and the salt stung the fissures.

And now, the perfect air, the moistest heat.

✦

When I first saw him, he scared me. When I saw him the second time, I figured I was hallucinating. This time, I want a closer look.

Alas, the man who works at the grocery store is on the bus again. The one who at first I was *sure* was Artan, but then absolutely positive was the teensy beanie guy, except with black marble eyes. Literally they are black marbles. They are evil but so without fear that he makes me wish I simply had what it took to survive on the same plane of reality as he, the zone far more beautiful and full of pleasure than the one I know.

I stare at him. He does not look at me. I'm not sure he can.

I look at him because he doesn't look at me. He will not look at me. Now that I'm living here I'm free but being seen feels like bullets. I understand that eyes will find me no matter what I burrow behind, but I aim never to bleed, only to observe, pretend, and consume.

Another swamp plus: among me are only creatures with no voice and no sex appeal. Creatures with gills and scales, feathers and shells.

The driver is careless and lets me ride the route in circles until night. I pull the wire. The bus stops. She says something to me before I get off. I ask her what she said—I want to see if she's scolding me.

She talks for a moment about her old friends. They all used to be real hippies, her included. But then the Beatles distracted everyone from the Vietnam war, and "everything was ruined, and from then on they were all fake hippies."

It's dark and thick outside. I imagine I can still see bands of rising steam from the asphalt, like a melanistic tabby cat. My arms almost feel cool, but it is only an illusion of the darkness. In bed, the water sloshing and massaging me from below the tarp, I think of the familiar face and marble eyes from the bus.

◆

I have a ziploc bag of cash and I decide to use it. I take the bus to a cafe for the wifi and watch decorating videos on my inactive iphone. There is one about color concepts that shows a room with string lights and green colors. I screenshot it.

At the store I find that man and choose his line. He rings me up for forty fresh potatoes, forty mini light bulbs, copper electrodes, zinc electrodes, a roll of wire, and an analog multimeter, and forty alligator clips. I can't bring myself to look at him while standing this close. The hair on my arms stand up. I say thank you, he says nothing, but I know he will.

I go to my room and wait eagerly for dusk.

✦

She doesn't know much about history, but she had a grandmother. She knows that.

There is much to escape from, and she has come to the wrong place. She now knows that, too.

She had only met her grandmother once. She was eleven, her grandmother probably near sixty-five.

✦

The water turns a special kind of verdant gold at sunset, and my stomach flutters.

I begin my potato project. I string all forty potatoes together with the clips and wire. I smush copper and zinc electrodes into each spud, which after forty leaves me with a raw divet on my thumb.

This is what I do when trying not to think about something: immerse myself in a project.

When all of the potatoes are equipped with two types of metal, I use my swiss army knife to cut a starter hole for twisting in the mini bulbs.

I thought I had forgotten the something, but here I am, stomach going from fluttering to clenching as night falls. I picture it: the veiny Hand with specks of algae in the wrinkles. Dew between the tendons. Green and blue veins diffused through gray skin into charcoal lines.

After I twist forty bulbs through mealy potato flesh, it's time to attach the two ends of the long potato line with a final clip. In preparation I test the electrical current with the meter. It should be buzzing, but not quite *on* yet. It's stronger than I expected.

Like the streetlights on a deep dark road activating at nightfall or the marquee of a restored theater lighting up again for the first time after years of neglect, bulb by bulb, my swamp illuminates.

The gold green water twinkles with light I've created. At the sight a sob catches in my throat.

◆

When I first arrived, I liked to play with the algae, swirling it around my fingers. Hours before the something happened, after I removed my fingers from the eye of my tiny green cyclone, I noticed little swimming aliens on my skin.

They were baby mosquitos, of course.

But I shrieked and flopped my hand around, limp like rubber, my wrist clicking, until the sticky silver things were gone. I can't tell you with confidence that it's not actually my own hand, in this ugly slack moment, that I've been seeing with my eyes shut.

Later that day I rode the bus in circles again. It was a standard day and was to remain so even if Marble Man got on, except it's *where* he got on.

Upon hour three of bus riding I prepared to get off at my stop. As the bus pulled to the sign nearest the lush little cove of vines and ferns leading to my swamp my stomach dropped. There a new shape. A deep sense of negative space.

He was waiting.

I was no longer tempted, as I usually was, to get a good look. I was, in fact, finally terrified of his supernatural eyes. His ambiguous face. Of his waiting on the other side of town in front of my home. I closed my human eyes tightly and stayed seated. I rode until the driver kicked me off six hours later. We talked more about pop music distracting the hippies from revolution.

That night I woke up sweating and screaming. I felt him there. My precious primordial lenses were gone. I was, once again, terrified. My swamp home was not mine anymore.

I did some diaphragm breathing and rinsed away my forehead sweat with green water. I told myself I was only afraid. That it was still mine. As relief began to trickle through me, I noticed the water level rise just a little, little more. Then, it came.

And it has come back four times since.

◆

She waits for the Hand to flop. Her ears perk in preparation for a gurgled scream, for bubbles with comma-shaped shine marks to appear under the potato lights.

It remains stoic. It mimics the cattails.

The great five-fingered cattail.

No body appears, as usual.

"I didn't move down here for that Great Depression cult," she says to the Hand, remembering stories her mother told her. Or, explanations, rather. Why grandma was so quiet. Why she visited only once, maybe twice.

It nods. Sort of.

"Also, this isn't a bog. You shouldn't be so well preserved," she says. "And we don't even know each other, so don't pretend this is some kind of metaphorical, familial type thing."

Though, they did hold hands, that one time they met. It nods.

The Tollund Man, found in Denmark, died in the third century B.C. The two brothers that found him thought he'd just died and called the police to report a murder.

They were not entirely wrong. Bog bodies often indicate violent deaths, as a bog is an excellent dump site. He seemed to have been hanged.

People've also found perfectly preserved butter in peat bogs. This clearly was a greater defiance of nature than well preserved butter.

◆

Hurricanes hit Florida in 1926 and 1928, causing The Great Depression to affect it before the rest of the states. In '29, a foreign fruit fly came to suck up all the citrus pulp.

Tiny, deflated basketballs hung from the trees. Black people could not vote and went to jail for standing somewhere too long, as it is today. Spanish moss made sweaty preteens itchy. Family annihilators killed their wives and children with 1855 Winchesters.

In April 2018, the government closed a Miami school called Rainbow Cultural Garden because it had ties to the NXVIM cult. They call it a sex cult. It's the one with the Smallville lady. The women were branded with a cauterizing pen.

Very MK Ultra stuff, if you ask anyone with an eye for context. Ted Kaczynski was an MK Ultra subject at University. The Manson murders were likely an MK Ultra situation gone way wrong. At the very, very least, very weird sex slave stuff, which is very US-esque.

"Danielle Honeycutt," she says. "That was it, right?"
It nods.

✦

The next day is too hot. She starts a new project, this time inside the store. She's going to do a Frankenstein type thing. She buys a power strip and a box fan. There's an outlet in the foyer, close to the automatic doors. They open each time she moves a limb.

First, she plugs the power strip into the outlet so that the metal plates suck electricity from the wall. Immediately prior to this moment, the electricity is the life-cloud.

Once absorbed by the metal plates, the electricity moves into and through the thin, metal strings encased by rubber. At this moment, the life-cloud becomes the juice.

The juice banks itself inside the square—where the outlets on the power strip live. At this moment, the juice reverts to life-cloud mode.

The fan is then plugged into one of the outlets on the power strip. The metal plates suck up the life cloud. The life cloud becomes the juice when it pours into the thin, metal strings encased by rubber.

And finally, the juice takes the shape of the fan. The fan is now alive. At this point, the juice is the fan.

It lives.

She sits in front of the fan.

✦

The Hand is in sepia Florida beneath wet sunlight. There's a fat, 600 year old treaty oak taller than most buildings in the 1930s.

I needed a new beginning.

The beginning I chose was the day after Priest Charles Coughlin's third ever radio broadcast. Eventually, he'd be kicked off the air for being too facist. Later, this would make no sense to me; all televangelists seem to be fascists. At the time, I did not know.

Three years earlier was S. Parkes Cadman, I think he was the first radio evangelist. If not officially, he's the first I remember.

Two years later, I hear Herbert W. Armstrong for the first time.

Georgia plugs the fan directly into a potato.

A sticky noise materializes. She knows what she will see when she turns around.

It nods.

"Hi," Georgia says.

Both blank spaces—the space before Georgia was born, where the Hand has life and Georgia has void, and the space that is this limbo state of wanting but not reaching Georgia—are each beginning. They have equal potential, whether one seems more formed than the other. Or more present. More alive.

It snaps and points. Georgia follows the finger to a sopping notepad at the end of her tarp. She holds the notepad out for the Hand to take and shivers as it slides from her fingers.

The Hand slaps the notepad against the water and it remains on the surface like the water is solid. Georgia blinks and it has a pen.

"Where'd you find that?"

It writes.

✦

Armstrong died in 1986, well before I did. By then, I didn't care about him. I had long departed from the Worldwide Church of God.

✦

I worked at a feed store, but customers stopped coming. As of today, I don't work at a feed store.

I move into the Oak.

From a hole at the base, I slither inside.

I sleep right in the middle of the gargantuan trunk. In the daytime, sunlight leaks through tiny holes. At night, it is pitch black.

On my fifth night moon beams pierce through the trunk and reveal spiders and larvae. When they move, the larvae sound like a human mouth smacking on peanut butter.

I stem upwards, hoping there will be an opening in the trunk near the branches. There is a small slit where the wood is thin and flaky. I break through moss and sleepy beetles.

The thickest branch is four times wider than my body. I close my eyes.

I build up a tolerance for oak leaves, since I can't afford food. I am surviving, but I am bored. I steal a radio and a potato from the kitchen at the nearby church. Then, I eat it raw. It powers me for an entire week.

Every Tuesday I steal a new potato from the church kitchen. It's usually empty. If someone sees me, they assume I am the help.

One Tuesday I am in the tree eating my potato, and I hear Herbert for the first time. Finally, someone talks how I feel. He says that we're entering worldwide famine. WWIII, too, probably.

To my pleasure, there's a phone in the church kitchen. I call in. The line is busy. The call becomes part of my weekly potato run.

I ring weekly for three months. Finally, I get through.

✦

"Hi," appears in thick letters on the notepad.

"So. What's up?" Georgia asks.

✦

Herbert loves me. It's more about that than the apocalypse.

I never meet him. We only talk on the phone. I have no money to send.

What are the true values in life? What is the way to peace, universal abundance and happiness? Those are the basic things we need to know! Those are the necessary things to know which man, science, technology cannot discover! Those are the things the Bible reveals.

On the radio, he talks lakes of fire.

On the phone, he says I need to abandon it all.

And again he says it, and again. The idea scares me. I've already abandoned it all. How can I do it again?

I ask him. He answers. Then, one day, women visit me. They knock on the tree base. I can't hear the knocks, but I feel the vibrations.

I don't answer because I'm not quite ready to do it, yet.

◆

When I finally answered the knocks against the tree trunk, they only reiterated what he'd already told me.

Then, "safety is the password," one of the women said.

I called him and said it.

"Danielle," he said warmly.

He said he'd ship the poison right after we got done talking.

I poisoned it, my own house, even though it was the oldest tree in the south. I used Velpar.

First, a patch of grass turned white. It wasn't until the rain that the white spots crept up from the base of the tree.

Townspeople left gifts at the tree. I still lived inside. They held a funeral. I still lived inside. I did not leave until after the highest leaves drank the poison, when the wood grew soft.

I moved into the decaying house where all the women lived.

I had no money, but he sent me gifts to the compound. I gave them to the tree.

One day I tacked a paper sack of jelly beans to the trunk. There I noticed a woman with long black hair. Her eyes were closed and her palms pressed against the wood. She hummed and traced the grooves with her finger.

Later, I saw her picture in the paper. She was a psychic who said that the tree was once an ancient Egyptian woman named Alexandria.

/ side b

CHARACTER IN FICTION

/ Gabriel Blackwell

Here's the character. Here they are. The character, he thinks, is the person who believes that a character in a fiction can be created solely via the act of choosing to quote some particular piece of writing, for instance, the third volume of Walter Kaufmann's *Discovering the Mind*, the one devoted to Freud, Adler, and Jung: "No single explanation can really explain human behavior; it can at most illuminate human behavior and allow us to see something we had not seen… An accident may be considered a paradigm. Why did it happen? The road was icy at that point. And the driver of the small car was in a great hurry because he was late for a crucial appointment, because the person who had promised to pick him up had not come. And his reflexes were slower than usual because he had had hardly any sleep that night because his mother had died the day before. And just before the accident his attention was distracted for one crucial second by a very pretty girl on the side of the road, who reminded him of a girl he had once known. Yet he might have regained control of his car if only a truck had not come toward him just as he skidded into the left lane. The truck driver might have managed not to hit him, but… If we add that the truck driver had just gone through a red light and was, moreover, going much faster than the legal speed limit, the policeman who witnessed the accident, as well as the court later on, might discount as irrelevant everything said before the three dots and be quite content to explain the accident simply in terms of the truck driver's two violations. He caused the accident. But that does not rule out the possibility that the other driver had a strong death wish because his mother had died, or that he punished himself for looking at an attractive girl the way he did so soon after his mother's death, or that the person who had let him down was partly to blame." The character, he thinks, is the person who created the character who thought that these thoughts, Kaufmann's thoughts, these particular Kaufmann thoughts, were worth reporting at some length—rather, in other words, than summarizing them, paraphrasing them, or even simply presenting them as their own thoughts—

though also a character who didn't think these particular thoughts needed any further context. The character is not Kaufmann, who is or was, after all, a real person and not a character. And also, it's important to say, the character is not the character who presented Kaufmann's thoughts without context. And the character is most definitely not him. Not me, he thinks, I write.

CRUEL, AND UNUSUAL

/ Gabriel Blackwell

Because this man is a writer, he can imagine many different kinds of cruelty, is able to imagine many cruelties, but this man also knows he believes he only really has the stomach, in the end, to realize one of these many imagined kinds of cruelty, that of writing (while of course recognizing that this one kind of cruelty may yet produce many further cruelties; a realist, in other words). It might be reasonable to assume this cruelty would take the form of writing about others in a critical or insulting way, but this man, because he has been a writer for some time and has been a reader even longer, this man understands that really the cruelty comes from writing about others in any way at all. What is it that might make this man, this writer, want to be cruel? Well, because this man is a writer, we know that it could be virtually anything at all, which is to say it could also be nothing at all. So, something. The man doesn't know what it is and so we won't know what it is. It's a difficult thing, the man thinks, to be a writer, when every act of writing is a cruelty. And because what this man began to write was fiction, and because his fiction was most often left unread by others, he understood before he'd even begun that what he was going to write would be a cruelty perpetrated against himself. And so he had a thought; he ought to leave this fiction he'd written in a place where the man he lived with would see it, because he thought the man he lived with would be curious about this thing he, the man this writer lived with, had found, and would then feel himself bound to read it. It may go without saying that this man, this writer, believed that the man he lived with would read the thing he'd found because this is what the writer would do under the circumstances. The world, though, is not arranged that way, and the man the writer lived with saw the writing the writer had done, and, thinking it was probably something the writer hadn't meant to leave out, something, in other words, that wasn't meant to be read by others, not even the man this writer lived with, he simply left it there, where he'd found it, without so much as picking it up—without, in other words, reading it. The writer waited weeks for the man he lived with to bring up what he, the writer, had written, but the man the writer lived with never did, in all that time. And so the writer had the idea to repeat the experiment, but this time, he would make the first word of his story the name of the man he lived with. In fact, he decided, he would name the main character of the story he was writing after the man he lived with. Even if the man this writer lived with thought he wasn't supposed to read this thing that he'd found lying on the table in the living room, if he saw that the main character had the same name as him, how could he not then read it?, the writer thought. The writer first thought he ought to write a story in which this character was a hero, if only so that he could get his way without also creating strain at home, and so the story started that way, but, after he'd written a sentence or two, it all felt so false to the writer that, in his next few sentences, he so debased, degraded, and embarrassed his character that really this writer felt he'd lost his way, in the story he was writing and in life, and so he stopped. Over dinner, the writer asked the man he lived with for his opinion: Should the main character in his latest story be a hero, or should the main character in his latest story suffer some horrible fate? The man the writer lived with, not being himself a writer, said, *Why can't it be both?*

HUG WITH A PLANT

/ Kim Ha-ri / trans. Kim Yong-Jae

It was on an overseas porn site early on Friday morning that Yun saw his sister's video. On the thumbnail was written in bold text "Leaked Video of Yuni Jeong, a Representative of the Sales Management Team 1 of Company A." His sister in the image was in a purple dress, smiling brightly at her ex-boyfriend. He only heard about that from her, but it was the first time he saw the video himself. He pulled up his pajama pants and logged out of the site.

He happened to find a site for the victims, while searching Google for revenge porn. The site name was SOO, short for Seeds of Oblivion. The creator of the site was also a victim of revenge porn. In the introduction to the site, she said that she was distributing seeds for free to solidarize with the other victims. She was saying that she would be happy to send a seed to anyone who wanted it, regardless of country, race, gender or religion by international mail. The purpose, but not a duty, of giving seeds for free was, she added, to share the process of growing plants on the site after receiving the seeds and to communicate with other victims.

Yun applied for a seed after introducing himself as a victim's younger brother. But "I can't tell you the news about my sister because she has not yet overcome her distrust of the Internet," he wrote, feeling a little bit sheepish. After sending the email, he pulled the blanket up to his forehead and stayed in the dark, and it suddenly occurred to him that even when the morning drew on, the world would still remain in black and white.

A month later, an international mail arrived from Lithuania. Dozens of blue stamps were postmarked, indicating that it had arrived via several places. Yun drank a sip of beer and tore open the envelope. A white card and a seed in a zip bag were wrapped in eco-friendly craft wrapper. On the card was written "To Yuni, with love from Lithuania." With love! Yun felt ironic and surprised because the people who mocked Yuni were anonymous, so were the people who shared love with her. Early in the morning the next day, he headed to his parents' house in Suwon to bring the seed to his sister.

After a brief meeting with his parents, Yun decided to take his sister to his house in Banghak-dong. His parents told of their plan to put his sister in a closed psychiatric ward. The moment they showed Yun the document of consent to compulsory hospitalization, he felt as if a part of his intestines had fallen off. What the hell fell off? He wanted to know what it was and its name. On the way to Yun's house in Banghak-dong, they did not say a word. Yun thought that Yuni's behavior, consistent with silence, could be justifiable. Snowflakes drifted wildly and grotesquely outside his car windows.

He arranged for Yuni to use a room facing the veranda. The room was the sunniest of all. He didn't want to use the room as it was too bright. Now that he thought about it, his hesitation to use the room might have been a harbinger for Yuni. Yuni unpacked her luggage and lay down on a mattress. He feared she would feel bored when she was alone, so he took out an iPad, a coloring book and colored pencils for her. Saying she didn't need an iPad, she added.

—Please find me a part-time office job.

That Monday Yuni started working at the desk of a delivery company. Her main job was to enter freight invoice numbers and answer calls for inquiries. When he woke up at 7 o'clock to go to work, he saw Yuni's leftover cereal and coloring book on the table. He opened her notebook and saw that she had painted flowers in purple. He thought of that color all the time he was welding in the factory, and even asked an office worker in purple-knit at a cafeteria at lunchtime, "Do you like that color?"

He worked as a welder in a factory making outdoor lights. After his work hours, he also took care of personal work for his boss. He did chores for his boss, such as fixing the hem of his cat tower, but he devoted most of his time to making products for sale on Etsy. Earrings and necklaces made from pieces of aluminum, sun catchers made from broken glass, dream catchers made by weaving cable ties and waste vinyl, and many more.

On the third day after working for the delivery company, Yuni headed to the veranda with a flowerpot and a plastic bag. She was laying newspapers on the floor and putting culture soil in the pot. He sat next to her and asked her what she was doing.

—I can't turn a blind eye to the gift from Lithuania.

Yuni smiled faintly just like before.

After work, Yun sat at the table and glanced at the SOO site. On the bulletin board, photos and texts of flowerpots were posted by victims living in the UK, Belgium, Hungary, Colombia, and Indonesia. There were also a few Koreans. Yuni might be one of them. He was sort of hoping that his sister would post on the bulletin board. What would it feel like if he, unable to sleep until dawn, logged in the site to find Yuni's post there?

He scooped out the leftover sake bowl with a spoon, and the rice was dry. He had hardly headed to the microwave when he heard the door open. Yuni from work headed to the veranda without even greeting Yun. He followed her, only to find that she was looking at her flowerpot on her table. Yun said she should stop work and take some rest. She said that if she didn't work, she would have a lot of wild thoughts. And then, she made her hands in the shape of a conch and talked to the plant, as if she were whispering towards it. There were quite a few posts on the bulletin board saying that they would talk to the sprouts just as Yuni did. It was just common and normal for them to talk with the sprouts.

A few days ago, he took on a custom order. Last time, he removed all the wood at the bottom of the cat tower and replaced it with a solid iron plate, which pleased the owner well enough to ask him to make a tree by twisting an aluminum wire. The art of an aluminum string, a real magic money tree. The boss instructed an accountant clerk to collect all the coins and give them to Yun Jeong, the head of the department. "Putting coins on branches would be cool, helping the company to thrive," he said.

The work was not as easy as he thought. He had to work extra three or four nights. The boss, satisfied with what he did, paid him with a bundle of cash. Yun went to a popular confectionery store near Banghak Station and bought a crepe cake. He wanted to buy Korean beef, but he didn't, thinking that his sister might be vegan. They'd been living in the same house for nineteen years, living apart only for six years, but Yun didn't know anything about his sister. He didn't know whether she was vegan or pesco-vegetarian, whether she liked reading or not, or who she voted for in the last election. He knew nothing about her, which was why this happened.

The clock tick-tocked towards midnight. It was quiet. His sister might have gone to bed right from work. He turned on the table lamp and carefully put the cake on the table. A sound was heard from the veranda. "I'm sure the door was locked." He tiptoed towards the veranda. The sliding door was half open. Yuni was climbing up the ladder and tying a rope to a clothes hanger installed on the ceiling of the veranda. Yun felt as if his heart were pouring to the floor. "You can't die! You can't die!" he screamed, and Yuni screamed back. She threw anything she could get at Yun, such as a rope, a spray gun, and a hoe.

—Why are you screaming like that?

Yuni turned on the light. He flopped down on the floor and looked around. He could see clean veranda windows and flowerpots, richly colored soil, and a long stem above the soil around him. The seed had grown quickly. He stood up, scratching his chin and pretending it wasn't a big deal. He felt a strange sense of distance about his sister throwing the hoe, but he thought he would behave like that if he were in her place.

The two looked closely at the plant. The hem of the stem was rather thick, becoming thinner as it went up. The tip of the stem grew to the point where it reached the clothes hanger, but it fell because of the difference in thickness between the hem and the tip of the hem. Yuni sneaked into the garden in front of the house and broke several branches. She said that she was trying to make a support by tying each branch with a rope. It was very fumblesome.

—You mean that you will do this with a rope like this? Yun asked.

She shrugged her shoulders and touched the stem of the plant. The color of the stem was unique. It had only a partial green, light green, or yellow color, which were all common in the botanical family. Thin veins were visible in the stem, and purple sap mixed with blue light flowed up and down. He asked Yuni what if she would post on the bulletin board saying that the seed had already grown this much. Yuni stared at him and gently slapped him on the shoulder with her fist, saying she didn't do anything vulgar like the Internet. Hoping to change the subject, Yun asked,

—Are you a vegan? I bought a very expensive cake, but it must have some milk in it.

—I love beef insoles,

Yuni answered, rubbing the back of her hand. She got a bruise on the back of her hand. At a delivery company, office workers like her might also have to help with the field work on busy days. She took out a cigarette and lit it, which would be sure to attract a complaint from the people upstairs. But he didn't want to stop his sister. Cigarette smoke danced high to reach the tip of the plant's stem. Yuni went to bed without taking a bite of the cake.

The next day, the thought of the supports for the plant came back to haunt Yun all the time he was welding. "How could I make supports for the plant to grow safely?" He thought it foolish to build supports with tree branches or something. After waiting for the other workers to leave work, Yun went to the pile of pipes he had collected behind the factory to sell to a junk dealer. He thought he could weld a few 1T thin pipes together to serve as a support.

Yuni said she decided to call the plant Anna. After installing the supports, Yun loosely tied a cable tie to each stem node. While knotting the tie, he wondered where she got the name Anna from. While googling before going to bed, he could find Anna Karina, Anna Nicole Smith, and Anna Pavlova, but he couldn't figure out what kind of relationship there was between these Annas and the plant... until he removed all the supports when Anna's stem grew firm and straight enough to stand on its own.

As the plant grew, Yuni had more wounds. One day, he came back home late and waited for her until dawn, but she just said that she had the wound on his forehead stitched in the emergency room. The only place in the house to talk to Yuni was on the veranda, so he couldn't ask her why she was hurt or if she was okay as she walked into her room with a bandage on her face. Except when she fed Anna plant nutrients on the veranda and made sure her buds were growing well. Besides, her answer was always the same whenever he asked.

—You bastard. Don't ask me. Shit,

she said with a cigarette in her mouth. She spat out swear words like fucking, scum, shut up, you son of bitch as well as you bastard. It seemed that she was not swearing specifically at her younger brother, Yun. Her cursing was directed at a target that could only be referred to as someone other than Yun. Yun had searched and read a news column every lunch break at his company since his sister started swearing. Typing in search words in the search box, such as "how to get out of trauma," "how to handle an angry mind," and things like that.

Then one day, he came across a column saying that growing plants can heal people's trauma. At the end of the column was written "Don't be overly considerate of them and let them go." He was worried about the cigarette smoke between the floors, but as long as Yuni could come back to her former self, he decided to let it go.

So, he believed in the efficacy of Anna and cigarette-smoking. It seemed to him that swearing by his sister was also a kind of positive expression. At least she had gone from keeping silent to talking to herself, from talking to herself to cursing. Anna's stem had also thickened and her new shoots had sprouted. She burst a purple lotus bud about three weeks after his sister came to his house. During his break, he googled color names. The Pantone colors were 17-3020 Spring Cross, 14-3207 Pink Lavender, and 13-0324 Letters Green. When he came back home from work, he wanted to let his sister know about this on the veranda, the home's official interview spot, but he couldn't.

The person Yuni beat was a man who lived on the 8th floor. Yun had never seen him before. Nor had Yuni. Yuni, who left work early, dropped by a flower shop to buy a large flowerpot, culture soil, and some nutrients for plants, and she stood waiting for the elevator. The man on the 8th floor asked her if she wanted him to help her with her luggage. "Do you know me well?" "Well, I know you. Everyone knows everyone else if they live in the same apartment."

—Where did you see me?

She didn't leave work early. Actually, she was fired. Anyone who made eye contact with Yuni or pretended to know her sounded provocative to her. She would ask them, "Do you know me?" "Where did you see me?" "You know me, right?" "Did you see me on a porn hub?" "Are you a porn addict?" Yuni tussled with anyone instead of just arguing.

Yun told the man that he could pay him the settlement money at a notary office soon. The man kept very calm, although his forehead had been struck with a flower pot. He didn't tell Yun to head to the police station. He didn't even wag his finger at Yuni. In his eyes, Yuni seemed obviously crazy and insane. It was rational that her parents wanted her to be placed in a mental health facility.

Yun kept thinking of that while pressing the password on the keypad. He was also a rational person. He had never beaten people like his sister did, nor had he ever done any harm to others. Still, he could not dispel his conclusion that it was normal for Yuni to show such violence. Her anger was the price of logical thinking. He was led to walk towards the front of the veranda even without realizing it.

Yuni was changing pots, with Anna uprooted. Anna's flower buds had grown quite large. Cigarette smoke danced in the shape of a thread around the flower buds. It will bloom at the right time of spring. When the flowers bloom, his sister will stop smoking. Yun did not forget a column on the healing power of plants. Temporary smoking would be no big deal. Outside the sleek windows, a tuned car radiated pink lights, illuminating the veranda slopes. It was not clear what the LED lights meant. Still, he thought it would be close to the axis of positivity. He slowly moved his gaze from the window to Yuni. She had stopped changing the pots and was poking Anna's stem with her shovel.

Yuni stabbed a lot of places on the plant. The wounds spread like a pattern all over the stem rather than healed. Yuni avoided Anna for a while. But three or four days later, in the morning, Yuni sat in front of Anna, touched her wounds and whispered. That day, she was waiting for Yun at the table when he came back home from work. It was the first time that she spoke to Yun again three weeks after coming to his home in Banghak-dong. "Can I work in your factory?"

—If I'm with Anna, she talks to me. I'm still so embarrassed that I can't afford to see Anna.

—Turn on the internet and watch only Job Korea and turn it off.

She looked at Yun and then chewed her lips.

—I can't. Please do it for me.

There was no probability that Yuni could find a job on her own because she did not use the Internet. Yuni ran away from the Internet. From the frame of the video in which she appeared, from anonymous viewers watching the video, from the ridicule born at their fingertips. She was hit and bounced off. Just like the law of nature. However, the self-employed chose to post wanted flyers on the Internet instead of putting them up at the entrance of their businesses.

Yun crossed his arms and leaned against the wall. He let out a sigh and said that he would talk about it with his boss. He saw Anna on the veranda. Anna's wounds grew even more to form a pattern now. It seemed that her scars did not disappear instead becoming permanent. Dozens of flower buds from Anna's branches bowed their heads. What color would it be when it blooms? What would the final color be like?

Yun had to build 1,300 outdoor wall lights to be shipped out a week later. It would take lots of time to assemble 1,300 products, but folding the packaging posed another problem. Field workers were too busy assembling to fold the boxes. The boss said it would be better for Yuni to fold the boxes and do some taping. Yun told the boss that he would not have to pay Yuni. The boss must have considered himself very lucky. Yuni headed to the industrial complex at eight o'clock on Monday in Yun's car.

There are people who avoid working in factories, while there are people who only work in factories. It is because of the characteristic indifference of the people who work in factories. The field workers seemed to have no interest in each other and to live in their own secret hut called an iPhone. They didn't pay any attention to Yuni's existence from the first day she went to work, and Yuni may have been thrilled and even felt grateful for that. Because no one in the factory was not aware of Yuni.

All she had to do was to fold small boxes at the factory in Building 1 and do some taping on their bottoms. She also put the products that the staff had assembled in the boxes and then sealed them. Every day, she worked from nine to six, changing five boxes of tape a day. She sometimes took out food waste, household waste, or carcasses of mice brought by a black cat that was fed at the factory into the firewood stove under the instructions of the site manager.

The firewood stove was located in the workshop of Building 2 where Yun was working. The stove was about one meter wide and big enough to heat the whole factory. He often saw Yuni moving her trash heap back and forth in a cart. During lunchtime, she carefully watched the fire flames swallowing, rolling, and chewing the squirrel carcass, making it elongate like a rice cake. She didn't take her eyes off it, even though the smoke made her cry. Every day without missing any single day. Expressionless, but somehow showing a lively energy. After lunchtime, when she returned to the factory in

Building 1, Yun looked around the stove and looked inside it.

The body of the squirrel was twisting and melting in the fire. When it was almost burned out, leaving only a part of an organ, it bubbled as if to bless the end of its life. Yun was worried that Yuni's life would be darker than before as she was holding a funeral every day, but he couldn't stop her from doing it. The experts said, "Let go of her." So he kept silent. He took Yuni's actions on the chin. He stopped by a notary office and wrote an agreement with the man living on the eighth floor. He gave the settlement money and bowed down to him and apologized.

As Yuni spent less time with Anna, their relationship grew closer. Yuni said that they had now cleared up the misunderstanding and opened their hearts to each other so they didn't have to speak in human language. She said that Anna liked to drink whiskey, to listen to music (she told me the name of her favorite singer, which was too difficult for Yun to remember), and to watch Netflix dramas. She said that Anna also had a favorite actress, which she was so shy that she wanted to keep as a secret.

He stopped by CU on the way home from work and bought bottles of Glendale and Balvenie. On such a day, Yun would also join them in their meeting. His sister was just sitting in front of Anna and turning on Narcos Season 3 or Bridgerton on the iPad, which was somehow fun nonetheless. Anna and Yuni laughed and talked until dawn. Yuni would sometimes speak out loud for her brother, who was not used to their own way of communicating.

—Anna. Think about the wounds I inflicted on you. About the shape of the wounds,

Yuni said. Yun poured whiskey into the flowerpot, carefully looking at Anna's stem. Her hair was also fluffy and smooth without being uneven. Yuni continued,

—I really like the factory. It's really fantastic to do the same thing over and over again.

He wanted to say "You're right. That's cool. You don't beat people because you're busy applying tape," but he bit his tongue and looked at Anna's wounds. Her wounds had healed, but the scars still remained to form a permanent pattern. The repeated patterns of the wounds seemed to have become Anna's own personality, just like a monogram of a luxury brand. Newly growing stems bore a pattern as if carved from the beginning. He poured the whiskey on

Anna, looking at her buds. Small petals of life that had just begun to hatch. He photographed the flowers with a camera.

Yuni became skilled in box making. She was fast enough to surpass the speed at which field workers assembled objects. However, no one praised Yuni. The factory was a lukewarm place dominated by "Looking good," "Living well," and "Getting by just fine" rather than by "Doing well." People who were working with a blank face neither smiling nor crying. People who went to work in silence and left work like wind. People who ate alone and took a walk around the factory during breaks or lay down on the sofa in the staff lounge to take a nap.

The boss himself was talkative. He only talked about himself. How great he was, how much his family loved the money tree that Yun built. It was only during lunch break that Yuni could ask about Yun's personal work. Yun was uploading the pictures of the flowers taken the day before to the Google image search window. Yuni was sitting down next to him after she put the sparrow's remains that the cat chewed and swallowed into the firewood stove.

—I wonder what you made.

He showed her the Etsy sales page. The sparrow on fire burst out. A skein of fire burning in the stove left a mark on Yuni's face. She looked at Yun's works throughout her lunch break. Following his lunch break, he checked the firewood stove after Yuni left for Factory 1. The sparrow disappeared. Only the sparks that bounced off the welding mask intermittently might be traces of the sparrow. The names of the flowers he found on Google were snapdragons, forget-me-nots, violets, and bougainvilleas, each of which looked similar to Anna, but were strangely different.

Yuni started sketching after work. She drew while sitting on a fishing chair stretched out next to Anna. Sometimes she was so much immersed in her drawing that she did not even touch the whiskey she'd poured. Perhaps she focused on sketching for about three or four days. Yun intuitively realized that Yuni had finished the sketch while meticulously packing the products to be sent to buyers in the living room on a weekend evening. Yuni said, "Do you think so?," looking at Anna with a bright expression and then stroking a pile of flowers. Then she took a deep breath, pouring the whiskey into the flowerpot, as if determined to do something.

Lots of flowers bloomed without Yun's knowing it. Hundreds of purple flowers came out splendidly toward the floor. It looked like a female figure bent over to wash her long hair. Touching his hair, he recalled what a German philosopher had said: hair was the first plant to grow on the human body. If a plant grows on his scalp, then isn't Yun himself is a plant? and if Anna can talk to Yuni, then isn't Anna also a human being? Yun came closer to Anna, scratching his head. He pressed his ear against Anna's stem.

If humans have traces of a plant called hair, wouldn't Anna have traces of a primate called a heart? He couldn't hear Anna's breathing or heartbeat. Instead, Anna's flowers radiated a purple luster. His socks turned purple. One or two withered flowers fell on his socks. He picked up the flowers that had fallen on the floor and threw them into the trash can.

The next day, Yun switched Etsy to Holiday Mode. The boss was so impressed with Yuni, who perfectly folded the boxes without getting paid that he tolerated Yun's personal work. It was at a perfect timing that Yuni asked him to materialize her sketch. She called it re-ification, or materialization. Yun thought of the Eucharist and grape juice he had received as a child at a church he had visited once or twice out of curiosity. They said it was the body and blood of God they worshipped. He didn't eat it because he felt it was cruel. Is the act of making the intangible into something tangible somewhat religious or cruel?

The two began reorganizing the sketch and working on metal crafts well after six o'clock until the radio broadcast hosted by Bae Cheol-soo was over. Yuni asked Yun to request songs of Western singers he was unaware of, such as Will Oldham or Jens Leckman, on a radio app. Their songs had never been played on the radio. She said she felt relieved that her loneliness was buried in the chat window, where her own requests were rising rapidly. At eight o'clock, when the radio program ended, Yuni threw a smoked cigarette into the firewood stove and watched it slowly burn.

Yun tried to analyze the sketch that Yuni handed over to him. He could not understand what it meant. He couldn't find a center point or contrast of the object. First of all, it had no narrative. If asked to make a sketch of a cat, we can get the hang of the cats we encountered in our daily life and history. However, Yuni's lump had neither any origin nor gender nor characteristics. He postponed the production and crafting for several days because he could not figure out what the sketch meant. "What the hell is this?" "What is it?" It looked like a malignant lipoma, or a crushed heart. The sketch was just a fragment, a still cut without a context. What had Yuni tried to capture?

He brought piled-up pipes or scraps of metal. He melted them or used a torch to melt them one way or another. He raised the torch's firepower to get the hardware to stick to the workbench, aero-brushed it, or tried taking it with an iron tip. He sanded it or did nothing to bring the texture to life, creating various shapes such as cones, rectangles and triangles.

Yuni smoked throughout the work while listening to a song on the radio. The objet Yun finally proposed was just like a cake made by someone with terrible cooking skills. Faced with the objet, Yuni stubbed out her cigarette on the floor. She stretched out her hands towards her work but drew them back. She frowned as if forcing herself to swallow a bitter lump and said,

—It's no wonder that you don't know.

Yuni and the entire factory were seen in black and white for an instant. The factory lights did not go out, and the moonlight was also refreshing. In a brief moment of black and white, he felt as if he had opened the first page of a book he had been longing to read. He tried to guess what the thing his sister had just swallowed meant. The hidden meaning of the material he could not name but had to make. Why did Yuni swallow a lump of abstraction instead of a sweet cake?

Yuni went to bed shortly after working overtime. Yun opened the balcony door with two bottles of whiskey. Anna's stem was smooth with a beautiful pattern. A feeling of awe or envy for the life that transformed the shovel wounds into a pattern came to mind. Once he happened to watch a video on YouTube saying that mixing two whiskeys tastes awesome. After mixing the two in a long glass, he slowly poured it into the flowerpot. He crumpled up in the fishing chair and looked up at Anna. Anna shone purple rays. The purple rays soon filled the whole veranda. The rays flickered, making waves. He grabbed the bottle and closed his eyes.

(No.)

A faint voice was muffled. "Is it Anna?" Just in time, the rays emitted by the flowers became intensely denser. The white walls seemed colored amethyst as if covered with purple wallpaper.

—No about what? What is it not about?

He gently touched Anna's flowers that drooped like hair. The flowers were hot. "Is it drunk? Is there a problem?" Something vibrated through the thick flower bushes so abundant that he could not see inside. Yun stood up and ruffled Anna's hair. One, two, three, four, and then ten of the gray lumps fell through the hole that Yun had just made. When he picked them up and looked closely, they looked like cat poop and a skull, both of which were not what Yun expected.

They were dead flowers. He put the dead flowers in his palm and looked intently at them. They looked similar to Yuni's sketch. If there were a form that fell out of her heart after the man she loved posted a video on the Internet and then posted an insult to an acquaintance that synthesized Yuni's face in pornography on Tumblr, then would it look like this? Yun squeezed the withered flowers tightly. A lumpy and sticky thing stuck between his ten fingers.

—No.

Anna's rays flickered. He was about to ask "Something wrong?" but stopped asking. Because it was someone else who said no, not Anna. He opened the window leading to the master bedroom. In the dark, Yuni was lying on the bed, saying "No! Absolutely no!" in her sleep. He quietly closed the window and then touched Anna's stem. What Anna are you? What's your relationship with my sister?

The next day, heavy snow caused all the employees to leave work early at 4 p.m. Yuni and Yun started working in Building 2 of the factory. Yun decided to use the remaining fifteen centimeters of lead after soldering a circuit. After hardening the clay, he carved a mold out of it. He didn't have to make it as elaborate as when making custom-made products. Instead improvisation was essential now. He looked across Yuni while digging out the center of the square clay with the blade.

She leaned on the workbench, staring at how Yun was doing his work. He rolled a block of clay toward Yuni. He also handed over the sculpting tools and oil for the bar inside the mold. She looked at and touched the crafting tools as she would precious jewels. Yun brought a stool and sat down next to the workbench. He put his cell phone on his lap and turned on a radio app. A song came out. "It's raining heavily in the city, it's raining on homeless kittens." Snowflakes about the size of a fist were fluttering outside the window.

"Why does snow always fall without greeting?"

Snow erased all the horizontal and vertical lines of the world, changing it into a 2D world. He could see a black dot waving in the foreground of white paper. The dot grew larger and moved faster. Yun sensed that he was seeing things. He simultaneously felt the weird joy of entering the world of Yuni, which he had been curious about until then. But the joy didn't last long. The black spot turned out to be a black cat that brought a sparrow. It brought a sparrow bigger than its head and sat down in front of the stove.

—Lead will cool down in just five seconds, so once it's formed, it can't be fixed. We have to melt it again,

he said, stroking the cat.

He put the pot on the work burner and lit it. The melting point of lead is 300 degrees. Yuni almost buried her head in the clay while making a frame. The cat threw down the sparrow against the wall… until it ran out of breath. The cat was making a sound of chewing its feathers. When he put a thermometer in the pot, it was close to 300 degrees. He started dipping the lead slowly. The lead began to melt. A smooth surface appeared on the pot as if a mirror had been applied to it. He picked up the pot and poured it into the mold Yuni made.

They counted to five in their minds. The sound of a cat chewing on the sparrow's skull and a butane gas commercial song on the radio overlapped rhythmically. When the clay was broken, a uniquely shaped object appeared. It looked like someone with his ribs exposed and a heart pulled out and stretched vertically. It looked just like a dead flower that Anna spat out from inside yesterday.

What she created was beyond the vessel of a poem or a novel. The congealment of Yuni's experience. A chunk of incomprehension. Something that can be sold to nobody and nobody dares to buy. He rubbed both hands on his pants and reached out towards the objet. He could feel its heart beat as he wrapped his hands around it. He imagined the depth and breadth of the beat. A space where there was no end and no beginning came to his mind. What could be the density and intensity of the empty space? Yuni may have lived there, in an unknown tunnel until now. He felt moss sprouting from the back of his neck. He took his hands off the objet and wiped off a cold sweat.

Yuni picked up the now-headless sparrow with tongs. She threw it into the wood stove, took her first piece and sat down in front of the stove. Yun also took a seat next to Yuni. As she fiddled with her cell phone which was playing the commercial, she watched the sparrows burning. Yuni placed her objet on her lap and stroked it. She hadn't even polished it, but it had a smooth surface. The intermittent reflections of the hearth flames seemed to bring life to and revive the elongated heart.

The sparrow's carcass burned, giving a lot of smoke. The two of them coughed without looking away. The full cat was dozing off at Yuni's feet. She did not miss any single process of the bird's body being scorched and crushed, even though she shed three lines of tears in her eyes with her eyes burning. The black smoke subsided. The cell phone battery was dead. After the smoke cleared, the objet turned even brighter. He neared the stove to take a closer look.

—Sister. You know this.

She got up and headed towards the stove. She threw the objet into the stove. She came back, sat down, and took out a cigarette. Yuni was smiling subtly looking towards the stove. Yun hesitated somewhat, then pulled out a lighter and lit it. Tears still welled up in the corners of his sister's eyes. Outside the window, snow flurries softened. The stove burned even bigger with lead.

It was around 11 p.m. when he parked his car in front of the house. He was so late because he had to wait for the fire to go out completely. His entire body felt hot and cold, as if his eyelids and nose and lungs were full of coal. He needed a drink. When he said that he was going to buy a beer at a convenience store, Yuni also asked him to buy a bottle of whiskey. She added that she had been drinking Glenfiddich since she was 20. It was the first request Yuni made of him. "My sister. You liked to drink." He bought some alcohol for the two of them at the convenience store, adding one whiskey for Anna. He felt hot and sore in his throat as he walked to the apartment after paying for his purchase.

When he opened the door, the living room was quiet as usual. A gentle breeze blew through the gap in the balcony door. He looked at Anna while watching the curtains roll up shaking. The purple flowers in full bloom looked just like a figure wearing a dress with a stunning pattern on it. Yuni whispered to Anna in a conch shape with her two hands. There was a rustling of her lips and tongue. Yun came out after washing his face with cold water because his eyes were sore.

After grabbing a can of beer, he took a sip and headed towards them. Yuni's eyes and nose were still gray with smoke marks. The tears that flowed over the soot made three long, transparent marks on her face. She whispered to Anna, "I got rid of it," and then she hugged the flower. Anna and Yuni were entangled in a hug, and it seemed as if they had been together from the beginning. Yun poured the whiskey into the flower pot. When he lifted his head and looked around, the purple rays that Anna had spouted were coloring the place. This place was not black and white any longer.

UNFINISHED WORKS

/ Emily Wallis Hughes

Made from my mother Katharina Ernestina Hughes's art writings

Leave me now in the autumn of the year—

I am awake now with a smile on my lips
I want to do something different

                              say something into

what is visual

what is   soft

I do not have to see everything

the way everyone else does

Look at what I see

I say

I see words gently rolling

on ludicrous hills

My 'I' recognizes this

pattern
as I sketch these
four reflections
and this leafless
tree
I pay attention
especially   to
the bark
and the lines it
makes

I've been sketching this tree for hours and I have just noticed
the cat hiding in the upper third of the tree
I do not have to choose between illustrating and interpreting;
my design is feeling
my illustration   feeling

I will not let the loud voices block me out
Even though they   keep at it

Today I am drawing
gestures and
spatial relationships

Brain to hand, I

can see what is happening there

It's not complicated:

Intuition: my 'I'
pouring fresh milk for your 'I'
What's happening there
That's what I want

I approach the canvas

                       I must be discreet

                                           I am not together

              Where are my
            mechanics

I am looking at one of my drawings from 1978

and Kandinsky, 1905–1910

I've forgotten what it means to be able
to recognize
one's own art

I am abstract

      still I can hear

a tiny little voice inside
of me   barely   audible   she
wants to speak

I want to hear that voice
Maybe then I will learn who
I am

I think that
today

I saw myself

in some negative space
and for a moment
along the edges of
my piece

Can I speak through limitation?`

I have no objection to unfinished works

lines of broken hurrying water:
  the science of composition

How do I know who the Adult is?
Spring flowers.

> I was just sitting!
>
> Morning—

The self-portrait for me
is a point of departure
It is everyday life
My child is growing up
and I have recipes to write
and laundry to fold

Today I set about decorating a small pumpkin
I don't know how long the process took
I enjoyed it
I wrote "pleasure" several times
In the end I did not glue anything on it
I ended up puncturing
a small hole in the center
of the pumpkin where
the stem was and
I inserted a couple of leaves
I saved the stem

SESTINA I

/ Bradley J. Fest

Phenomenology does not suffice.

—Gilles Deleuze, *The Fold*

Satellite pulses reassess the time
of patiently hovering above things
wading toward some island conspiracy:
album art weakly given into hands
blistered open by rays of blinding light
obliging everyone to gather desert

forever. Alone, stalking a desert
miracle over the horizon of time,
sentient waste deposits shoulder light
burdens exclusively composed of things,
crumbs of matter encrusted on shy hands
while the dust confirms no conspiracy.

The last time critics talked conspiracy,
they held a convention in the desert
and it was a river of sun whose hands
strafed the pliant walls of narrative time.
No one could summon any compact things
to tell it differently—by any light.

It was enough to permit some stray light
to heedlessly scatter conspiracy
theories indeterminately toward things
better left forlornly in the desert
tripping across sound's metronomic time.
Or, at least, that is what the old hands

felt—children once delivered by soft hands—
though the almanac shed a different light.
This was the advantage of clock time:
an allergen become conspiracy,
an escape, respite, personal desert
for amassing tattered and shopworn things

within the underglot. And somehow, things
went on apace. Collectives joined hands
across old-growth forests, brand new deserts,
and some even played into fading light.
The violent tears of the conspiracy
ceased, permitting care, if only for a time.

These things happened in the future's desert
on which our hands rest, a conspiracy
of light staying our eviction from time.

SESTINA II

/ Bradley J. Fest

Le cimetière immense et forid, sans horizon,
Où gisent, aux lueurs d'un soleil blanc et terne,
Les peuples de l'histoire ancienne et moderne.
—Charles Baudelaire, "Une gravure fantastique"

Repetition's brush with a century's wan shape
stranded pilgrims on echoless shores of nothing
re-presented, so tradition held, as novel work,
a lexicon beyond speech's limits preferred
over a bewildered stare past a history
without corresponding archive. But these children,

difference's innocent babes, these time children
demanded new words and there were none, just the shape
of a reference gloaming out of history.
There were other modes of iterating nothing,
returning to the humorless thunder preferred
as portraits favor blank canvas, setting to work

painting preference, hazardous affective work,
but the dictionary mocked their efforts. What children!
Undiscovered words, such as *transudate*, preferred
other company, dismissing attempts to shape
arpeggios pleasant or astonished—nothing
so much as logorrhea bouncing off history,

which there wasn't much of anymore. History
had become effortless, inscrutable work
gathered fully and entered flatly from nothing
into the geobase, from children into children
as featureless seas among buildings in the shape
of drab pop-art icons the poets once preferred

over customary subjects (they now preferred
that careless evacuation of history
barely registered as prayer, redundancy, shape
without qualities, dissolution, work, work, work).
The record was not intended for the children;
it was made from nothing for no one toward nothing.

Shapeless, it was a placeholder for the nothing
historically guaranteed but not preferred
by the failed revolution's hidden children
secure from the prying mind of the history
narrated by lax copy editors to work
different dynamos, repetitions, a shape

obscured, an unquantifiable nothing-shape
preferred beyond itself for what used to be work
but is now just children carrying your history.

SESTINA III

/ Bradley J. Fest

Omnia fert aetas, animum quoque; saepe ego longos
cantando puerum memini me condere soles:
nunc oblita mihi tot carmina.
　　　　　　—Virgil, *Eclogues*

Architecture lingered. Sustained by a concern that an emphasis on
　　stratigraphy had vacated the years
of shedding disappointments previously "held to the whole," the
　　practice hesitantly focused on smaller, digital
units—less mammoth fallout shelters than locally-sourced rebar
　　and unadorned molding—easy to mistake at night
for drafts of moonlight or equinoctial turnover lines, things lacking
　　their own ostentatious music:
symphonies in the spheres, ballads in the pit, diseased breakdowns
　　on the stage—all the trappings of youth.
Left with a lone inharmonious guitar, the construction crew re-
　　moved sheets previously papering over the reality

of "already standing *within* it" to play minor pop from, to erect
　　baroquely detailed dioramas upon. It was one possible reality,
perhaps more personal than public, inverting on music stands an
　　objectivist condensation of miniature structures years
in the making—tiny subterranean metropolises collectively ignor-
　　ing the bombast and poverty of their species' previous youth—
for neutral scales, blank sizes, imperceptible comparisons with an-
　　cient metro stations, scotomizing androids, featureless digital
ubiquity sliding into the unhorizoned etiological doxing of any
　　"thoughts' torsion." It sounded like . . . lost music.
Toneless and arrhythmic, but nonetheless lyrical, the unmarked
　　vacuity persisted for a moment, two, but couldn't resist the
　　night,

its necessary sonority and unbecoming: the celestiodysmorphic
　　cruciate lune of repossessed drum machines. Facing perpetual
　　night,
the discipline decided once more to reassess itself, gathering its
　　still-breathing participants inhaling their reality
(as inoculation against their temporary laborers') to happily re-
　　mind themselves of ill-tempered music
repeating the structure of crescendos (verse/chorus) across so
　　many distorted minutes, years
(if being honest) of the same jam band pounding out the same
　　overtaxed solos, oblivious to other, digital
alternatives independent of concrete, steel, or stone *chora* mar-
　　ried to vaguely modernist song. It was imperative to hide these
　　activities from the straightedge youth

crews and to obscure as yet undrafted plans for broadcasting really,
　　really ambitious multiyear stories of surprisingly well-adjusted
　　youth
across the planet one excruciatingly colorful and self-referential
　　crossover episode at a time, night after night,
until absorption approached its subliminal limits, or at least, this is
　　what the purveyors of all that utopian digital
baloney hoped to concoct. If armies of poets hadn't long ago been
　　infected by the architects' reality,
translating it into serial after very, very serious serial long poem
　　prolonging the monotonous masculine notes through the ash-
　　phalt years,
perhaps other protests might have registered (though the preser-
　　vation of album leaves and compact-disc inserts preserved at
　　least some space for [the] genuine "music").

Fixing all this, however, staying its stillness amidst motion—un-
　　perturbable, inviolate, stationary (so rather unlike music,
if truth be told)—in a generation's discographic mind assumes that
　　these last years' faint sapphiric youth,
their not-all, their rarefied demographics, are subject to the risk
　　assessments paranoiacs have been impetuously carting out for
　　years:
that the spectral forces gathering in the gutters of the internet, the

hyperstereomyth for the planet's approaching night,
can convince (your) legions of prospectless offspring to affirm
    their isolation as the imposed precondition of their abstemious
    reality,
when they aren't, when they can't. No matter the hypebeasties
    lauding this or that new digital

affect, the kids are engineering a discrepant architectonic (or so
    they've always said), reautoformatting the digital
scrutiny monotonously imposed on their sonic *hrepenenja* (a long-
    ing for their antecedents' uncomposed music)
and scorning the "stricken punditocracy" (or so they've always
    tried). At least, these are some of the moves laid out in their
    new dance, a skipping, tripping reality
the engineers have already co-opted. And so it goes (again). Move-
    ment amidst crisis reveals (again) a youth
antevernal to necessity, left waiting on the heath to watch modish
    absolutes emerge from the night.
And so here they are, like before, but not for much longer now,
    facing down the years:

they haven't even aged a day, accumulated even one superscript
    past their most vital apex, these aphonic digital youth,
before they're brushed aside as just more elevator music, a monot-
    onous and overfamiliar requiem heard past every night
into yet another ploddingly dull morning when, finally, the real-
    ity that had already been chosen for their fate well in advance,
    despite a number of sincere appeals, would expire, succumb-
    ing at last to all those weary years.

AUBADE AND AFTER

/ Bradley J. Fest

J'ai seul la clef de cette parade sauvage.

—Arthur Rimbaud, "Parade"

Some mornings, when occluded light strikes your spines
            in a minor key and the sun's insubstantial rhythm
      fails to pulse on my leaden cheek or register its antique concern,
fading weakly into the flexing ambivalence you threaten to deliver
                        from the depths of seeming abundance,
I decide to support my commitment to your ongoing wonder
      with a catalogic patience
you cannot quite bring yourself to deny
            no matter your robust menageries and their heaving.
(Or at least, this is what my aspirant agents
      tell me
when they decline to quell your exhalations.)
                        Later, the valley's floor struggles to coalesce
around the weight of dissolute snowfields
            indexing each granule of my pointed regret.
The pirouetting Earth has little regard for such harlequinades,
      yet your parchment costumery confounds my attempts
                        to organize reflection.
The sun stands confident now,
      uprooting at least this contrapuntal performance's
languid reading practice;
            it dazzles the pines, their roguish silhouette
distinct against the penumbra of glassine memory radiating
      from the untouched ice-melt bounding the skyline.
   Lonely sentinels
                  absorb each cherubic ray
with their transiently reproductive covering and dutifully conspire
      against the neglected volumes
held in reserve;
                  the roofs—between which, at least from this height,

nothing seems to exist—overhang anonymous citizens penning
                              slim tragedies
all day, eventually weeping, eventually celebrating the fortress
    of their incapacious minds, eventually expiring from want of
material
    and then being immediately resurrected into the glare
of yet another sun and yet another day and yet another city
                    upon which some others will
                attempt to inscribe at least a partial
    record of your insurmountable
totality, you magical beast, you impossible library!
            What more do you want?
I vigorously hesitate to condemn or applaud these actions,
    for an event,
if you are anything, is something of an empty salon
                        leaving behind only the barest
    indication of potential clues that glitter then shadow
in their prodigious undecidability.
            When, for a moment, it fleetingly outpaces
                    the management-cult of reality,
lyrica beseechingly turns to you and others
                with a challenging request for numeration,
haunted by its unquenchable variety from which I again
    leap free, its cascading
                        and droning mathematics
livid against the mute biological fullness of your textual breathing.
            The lyric, in its brief (then ruined) multitude,
    aspires once again to a dawn I can no longer pinpoint
now that the stridency of the day's subsumption of grateful
    laminate rotation threatens all the homes below
my hilltop window;
            with your help, it sidles up behind me, taunting
and distracting—yet a blank
                    off-screen caesura—while
    I engage witlessly
a few particularly desiccated moments of collective history
                with no discernible rigor.
The sun now bores the sky and the people and I
                        doom by inattention

your most obvious lessons to sibilant erasure,
a rattling sorting
            of each stridently unbendable page
                              I refused
to read the first time. Past noon, some happiness is
      measured
by your tired bibliographers.
                        The sun's glare tuned
for the thinnest moment to a major key that those
      seeking some, any melody
could still not quite appreciate; meanwhile, elsewhere,
                  an ancient water main
bursts and with its quotidian flood the pessimism of
                              this hour,
                        and every hour from now on,
drags again across your lines and days
                  each sentence caught forlorn by
      the petrified ease of another morning while I
neutrally pace
      the afternoon and its unquilted promise. Other nights,
later, too soon, always on the cusp of some unconscious, accidental
                        departure, I would write, crossing the chance
convention of your sometimes invisible boundaries
      with ecstatic inattention
            while the cadence of your riffling revenant leaves speaks
      arpeggios and trilling arguments.
Eos ascends once more and you look different; again, your things
                        open auratic vessels of grimacing worlds
                  and animal tenderness, dilating
      tentative assurances
athwart the harmonious interstitial darkness descending
                  from dwellings metamorphosed into captured words.
      Today, I steal and ignore grunts and old saws for my
                              respirant codicils.
My embrace of residual unburdening belies the cooperating
      machines' stellar ambitions. Can you resist the violent imperative
                        of paradisal completion
and actually, tomorrow, touch
                  with fibrous vellum and translucent tendrils this

unconfirmed space,
assessing its veracity and fidelity?
I have a variety of solar concerns.
Regarding the possibility of enunciating
days that have not yet broken, you have contemplated at great length
their alien schism with tenacious overfamiliarity, but your focus
on strict alphabetization
returns even forgotten forebears into the fold of a staunch
presentism.
I might offer a closely-held self-portrait if you
assure me it will not double and triple back, reassessing with slight kicks
attempts to fix the plinth upon which your various tomes
would be mounted
to the hardscrabble sea-floor
(and around which untold ancient treasures would lay undiscovered,
lost icons of antiquity unbelievably covered in the
centuries' slow coral),
for I fear the traceless effacement of my insincere demotic confessions'
absorption into the monumentality of your ceaseless
motion. If I act, can you? And can your own action
void mine?
Even later, again, after indeterminately many mornings
spent reckoning the false horizon of memory
and continuity,
I awake as fragments, a meager representation of your daily influence,
but not lost, not floundering, just reassembling, again,
to walk and listen and do before midday once more asserts your
impossible claims on my attention
and the preposterous mirror you provide of the stars
spinning out their longevity
to so many other aloof audiences. The interval between
the story neither of us
can ever want to tell knows nothing of grace
or forgiveness or innocence but persists impossibly
in this mode
of light instrumental interlude, weakly performing our worldly
attractions and progressions.
We will enunciate another forenoon in which
we mistake

the barest outline of some cleverly substantial structure
　　　　　　obscuring the hesitant riddles we instinctively
　　collect to extend our basic capacities
a bit longer
　　　　for our mutual dependence. But then again, some morning
soon I may yet elude your albaic grasping, resting my hand beyond
　　　　your shelves upon things you helplessly let pass.

PENULTIMATE CARCASS OF NOMENCLATURE WITH CHILD
/ Nora Hikari

IN A MOMENT OF WEAKNESS I MIGHT BIRTH AN AUDI-
ENCE / AN APOLOGY FOR AN UNFORGIVABLE THING IS
ALSO A KIND OF UNFORGIVABLE / ERUPTING CHASMS A
WELL OF GRAVITY AN EXCESS OF ANGULAR MOMENTUM
/ A SHARP TAP AGAINST THE SOLAR PLEXUS BEHIND A
FIRM POINT OF CONTENTION / I AM A CONCENTRATED
BEAD OF REGRET AGAINST A SOFT BALCONY OF FOAMY
INDIFFERENCE / WHEN I ASK YOU TO LOOK AT ME IT IS
ONLY IF YOU PROMISE TO LOOK THROUGH THE WRONG
END OF THE TELEPHOTO / SO SMALL AND SO FAR AWAY
FROM YOU / ONCE AND ONLY ONCE I TOOK THE HAND
OF A YOUNGER SELF / BUILT FROM BRIGHT AND FLARING
TRUTH / PRESSED IT TO MY BLOATED SPINE / AND SAID
FEEL / FEEL WHERE ALL OF MY AVID AND TURGID DENI-
ALS HAVE BURST FORTH FROM / LIKE AN ILLEGITIMATE
RICTUS OF BASHFULNESS / TWELVE KITCHENS WEPT OUT
OF MY CHEST / ONE FOR EVERY FISHERMAN / FULL OF
LADLES AND SOUPS AND SOUS CHEFS AND ENOUGH SALT
TO SWALLOW ALL OF MY LATE GRANDFATHER'S AILING
HEARTS / AND ALL I COULD DO WAS STACK PLATES / I
SAW A MAN GIVE BIRTH TO A DRAWING OF A PARACHUTE
IN CHALK MARKER / AND ONLY THOUGHT ABOUT A
SICKLY WORLD FILLED TO THE LIPS WITH ARTIFICIAL
TRAGEDIES / LOOK HERE WHERE THE WATER LAPS AT
THE ROCKS / AND THE MOON JELLIES SLIDE IN TRANQUIL
DECAY / THE LITTLE CRABS HAVE NEVER FELT WARM
IN THEIR ENTIRE LIVES / THEY HAVE NEVER FELT SOFT
WITHOUT KNOWING THEY ARE SUDDENLY CLOSEST TO
THEIR INSIDES / BEHOLD THE MOUTH / THE ROCKFISH
CRAMMED FULL OF ITS OWN GULLET / BURST BY ITS
OWN SUDDEN ASCENT / THIS IS WHAT I MEAN WHEN I
SAY OUTSIDE PRESSURES ARE REQUISITE TO LIFE / HOW
THE CLIMB TO HEAVEN IS ACTUALLY WHAT KILLS YOU /

WHEN I WAS ELEVEN YEARS OLD I COVERED MY BODY
WITH POWERS OF TWO / THINKING THEY WOULD SMEAR
ME BEYOND MY BORDERS / THINKING THEY WOULD
TURN ME INTO A KIND OF NUMERICAL KUDZU VINE /
ETERNAL LIKE CHILDHOOD OR METASTASIS / WHEN I
WAS THIRTEEN I COLLECTED KNIVES AS A UNIT OF MEA-
SUREMENT TO UNDERSTAND THE SIZE OF MYSELF / MY
ARM IS ONE BLADE MY HEART IS TWO MY NAME IS A HALF
MY FINGERS MY WRISTS MY DELICATE BOYHOOD / AND
I MADE SURE THE BLADES FOLDED / IN A DIMINISHING
ARITHMETIC / HERE WE ARE AMONG THE ROCKS / HERE
AMONG THE LEAVES / HERE AMONG EVERY OTHER KIND
OF IMMORTALITY / AND ALL I WOULD SAY IS THAT I AM
GLAD NAMES WERE NOT FOUND IN THE WILD / BUT IN-
VENTED ONLY AFTER THE DISCOVERY OF SIN / SO THAT
UNLIKE EVERYTHING ELSE IN THIS UNIVERSE / THEY HAD
THE GENUINE CAPACITY TO DIE

/ **Simon Perchik**

With the door gone now
you set out for the waterlogged
as if some makeshift plank

could face shore as a stone
already upright, filled
with branches and salt

though there's no sail
and even more than the sea
you have no place to mourn

—you need driftwood :a mask
held in place by an emptiness
certain it arrived before you.

/ Simon Perchik

This stone was never in love
though you are now its Spring
—where there was no one before

you bring it rain, grass
and one by one an afternoon
no longer the hammer blows

it returned from—you send it
pieces, edges, embraced
in the dirt that lasts forever

wants to become a sea again
and this stone spreading out
with you in its arms, naked

then whole—was never so new
soft and against your forehead
here the flowers will close.

/ **Simon Perchik**

You lace one shoe with thread, the other
as if this wooden spool could be held
spin end over end and hold you

by the hand, let you feel her body
no longer moving as the careless tug
in all directions at once—you learn

to limp, to hear dirt struggle
and the step by step as if it could escape
not yet leaching in your hands.

LADY OF THE CANAL

/ Mary Biddinger

We're on Lake Shore Drive, in one of those SUV taxis with flames painted on the sides. Next stop: every museum, followed by the architectural boat tour only booked by tourists with zero knowledge of architecture. Under the blue awning, riverside, I crack a joke about "Wacker Drive." My outfit a cross between accidental soft butch and academic drifter. Overalls pocket stuffed with food co-op receipts. Boots a little too industrial. My roommate is dressed as a French nanny who smokes Djarums and speaks shockingly proficient English. We leer at couples redeeming coupons torn from the Entertainment Book. It's probably a two-drink minimum. Back then nobody looks at their phone unless placing a call. I worry that I forgot to wear deodorant, then brace myself against a bench, laughing. My roommate pesters the captain with targeted questions about the *SS Eastland* disaster. He's disquieted, but into it. A waterlogged pair of sweatpants licks the gangway. We're code switching into French, then heading to the bathroom, which is more like an ice fishing shanty. I'm peeling off my corset while guarding the door. My roommate and I swap wigs, and I become a silver blonde who owns a speedboat named Lady of the Canal. In the distance: hairy thigh of the Swissôtel, where someone's husband drops his watch into an ashtray, unbuckles his belt while thinking of me. We've exceeded the two-drink minimum and I order a cider, having no knowledge of which kind fits my persona except *hard*.

A VERY DECENT LIFE

/ Mary Biddinger

A cat can have a very decent life in an apartment, especially with roommates who compose regular fan letters to the wild salmon vendor. I was hogging the bathtub again, so my roommate ran downstairs to the restaurant to use their outlets. We were heading to Venetian Night to see the illuminated boats and talk tourists out of being patriotic. Did they think it was a festival of miniblinds? Did they reckon the El was short for elephant? My roommate had been to Italy so many times that the anecdotes blurred into one psychedelic slideshow of tangling with strangers on the subway and shopping for antique shoes at dawn.

A cat can have a favorite roommate, and technically ours did not, but she only bathed with one of us. When I first moved to Chicago I was really concerned about things like grout coloration and sharpness of my pedagogy. Two years in, and I was letting students dig through my purse for entertainment while we spatter-painted some flocked wallpaper and called it multimodal discourse. One day I was really down: somebody had called me "dizzy" as an insult, and I started sobbing right there in the seminar room. But then my roommate ordered an assortment of balloons delivered by "singing cow" to the main office, where I was second-guessing the firmness with which I'd filled out my final grades triplicate form.

I felt like an incomplete bubble pressed with a dull pencil as I made excuses into the phone to prevent my stupid boyfriend from meeting us at Venetian Night. Impromptu shellfish allergies, gnat warning, premonition of pickpockets who targeted former quarterbacks turned literary theorists. It was rough out there. My roommate finished buckling our cat's sequined peacoat, and we stomped out the door with our dignity.

ADVENTURES OF MARY VAN PELT

/ Mary Biddinger

I don't know, *was* the short story about me? Delilah stormed out of workshop and our professor groaned, reached for his thermos of prosecco. Delilah returned to stuff pages one through twelve into the garbage can. The story was accidentally single spaced. A water stain spread across the south wall of the seminar room, a moldy island. Karl chased after Delilah. I'd brought half a dayold yellow layer cake to class with me. Feather glanced at her violin case. That was the day Meg wore shades to workshop for the first time. It was early enough in the new year that I was still "trying." Black and white striped tights with garters, metal lunchbox purse, hair flat-ironed on all sides by my roommate, who could level anything. Michael was fiddling with his unflavored Chapstick again. Good thing I'd decided against my t-shirt with "Denouement" across the chest in gangbanger Old English script. The clock was permanently stuck at 8:05, but the second hand kept rotating in stabs. A surge of worry when I realized we'd forgotten to detach the massive adhesive eyelashes that my roommate had been peddling along with unpasteurized dairy products and hemp rock candy. I was blinking uncontrollably as the professor launched into a musty sermon on the downsides of verisimilitude. Couldn't help but read the first paragraph of my story again, albeit upside down. Is it possible to be the heroine, and the villain, in your own work of fiction, but unintentionally? Bob was our closest thing to a creative nonfiction writer, and attended class so infrequently that we joked he wasn't even real. The lights flickered a little. Suzanne coaxed open her bento box of snap peas, but the entire thing erupted like a canned snake, and Charlie screamed. Since Twitter would not be invented for another eight years, at that very moment Delilah sat in the computer lounge drafting a listserv manifesto about thinly-veiled autobiographies masquerading as literary fiction.

THE PROBLEM OF SUMMER

/ Mary Biddinger

My roommate never mourned a semester's death, just banished teaching blazers and swabbed every piece of a stolen office phone with rubbing alcohol. We had seventy-two hours between final grade submission and full time employment as office temps, clerks, or bouncers, or working the translation hotline, which took me beyond the comfort zone of my French. Twelve hours to leave the bottom page of the grade triplicate form on the dining room table before filing it with takeout menus. Utility bills roiled like a haphazard crock pot stew.

Days earlier, students lined the hall outside my office fetching portfolios, sharing sticky blue candy and unicorn erasers, occasionally a mixtape or melon-scented candle. Afterwards I cried into my hair in the elevator. Looked at the sky and the sky gave me the finger. Blocks away, corporations awaited a new receptionist to really mix things up, someone with an eye for organization who was also an eyeful. At home, my roommate answered the phone with an inscrutable patois. Long distance callers debated myriad connotations of the word *stalk*.

We had the luxury of two phone lines in our apartment, but the ring sounded the same for both. The phone instruction booklet was green and saddle-stitched, relic of a bygone era. Every button had only one purpose. Nowadays we might call it *midcentury chic*. Our apartment was too hot for fans, not hot enough for the rattling air conditioner that dangled from a window like a drunk tourist. Calls shuddered through the night in six different languages, and even with the ringer turned down I woke every time my roommate picked up.

Some of my friends were married and got to spend summers on a front porch with a pitcher of lemonade, wearing skirts for comfort rather than tips. Certain boyfriends tended other people's high-end teardowns, sipping Rolling Rock in the bathroom. A nemesis of yesteryear penned a casual memoir about a yacht named *The Debbie Gibson*. My roommate slammed one verb conjugation cheat book onto another. Neither of us considered solving the problem of summer with a one-way train ticket or a rich old man.

THE LITTLE HALFWIT

/ David Welch

a translation for Jack Spicer

It wasn't late
but was after
noon & leaving.

It left a useless
little
shrug.

A statue
played with
what remained.

Shadow of
the other fruits,
none stayed

clothed. Time is
only, was a joke.

A DIAMOND IN THE UNIVERSE

/ David Welch

a translation for Jack Spicer

A howl of hairless dogs screams from the branches.

A dog killed the moon.

A howl of hairless dogs scream.

A seagull eyes the womb.

A LANGUAGE OR BARRIER OF LOVE

/ David Welch

a translation for Jack Spicer

The nose is a simple machine

we learn to speak under

THE NEWS

/ David Welch

a translation for Jack Spicer

The river talks to its new neighbors.

It sweeps its current events to their doorstep.

A child, wounded like a pheasant

fallen between two towers.

A St. Bernard carrying lilies in his barrel.

A wine cellar hollowed into the floor

of a moss-covered cave. White water

worn through the mountains.

TANKA

/ David Welch

a translation for Jack Spicer

The gulls lease their homes
from the power company.
Beneath them, you try

to impregnate the sand, wind
knocking the wind out of you.

MESSAGES SENT IN THE SEVENTEEN HOURS OF THE DEFECTIVE RAT
/ Marcus Pactor

(TO THE GENERAL MANAGER OF PETSMART STORE #3571)

I am writing in regard to the defective rat I purchased from your store this afternoon. I have not been surprised that, as an opening play for dominance, my three veteran rats have taken turns mounting it and thrusting their hips in a frenzy of pseudo-intercourse. But I am sorry to report that the rat you sold me has not once attempted to mount or squirm free of a veteran. It has squeaked. Its squeak sounds like the squeak of a chew toy which has endured the teeth of every stray dog in the neighborhood.

Also: have you ever had in stock one hundred rats with their tails knotted together? Internet reports call their rabid total a "rat king."

(TO THE HEAD OF RESEARCH AND DEVELOPMENT AT EA GAMES)

My daughter and her boyfriend would likely enjoy a video game in which a rat king threatens to rape and eat a scantily clad woman lost in a maze of sewers. The condition of their minds is such that they would intentionally fail to enter the sequence of buttons necessary to save the woman even if she was also the President of the United States and the scene was a less-than-secure bunker under the White House.

(TO THE PRESIDENT OF THE UNITED STATES)

I doubt you have been briefed on the kind of YouTube clip in which a human is filmed while playing a video game. This travesty of entertainment is popular among humans with a peculiar condition of mind. I am concerned that a subset of humans who share this condition of mind may be streaming these YouTube clips at such a death-level volume that their fathers cannot tell whether they are genuinely enjoying the clips or the clips are merely providing noise to cover the breathy grunts of their intercourse.

(TO THE GENERAL MANAGER OF PETSMART STORE #3571)

The veterans see through the defective rat's fur to the weakness of its heart.

They wrestle and race on every floor of the cage while the defective rat slinks into a red plastic house where it can suck air in peace.

(TO THE HEAD OF RESEARCH AND DEVELOPMENT AT GENERAL MILLS)

I am writing in regard to your company's recent addition of black worm marshmallows to Lucky Charms cereal. The marshmallows in Lucky Charms have always been based on colors found in rainbows, so the inappropriateness of black is too obvious to merit analysis and rebuttal. And the marshmallows' shapes have always replicated inanimate lifeforms. One of your more geekish marketing strategists could probably cite an obscure legend or three in which worms and even more outlandish forms of animate life were employed as charms, but that strategist knows as we all know that worms forebode worse than clovers and moons.

(TO THE MAYOR OF JACKSONVILLE, FLORIDA)

I am writing in regard to the giant oily surface that has spread over a section of the bike trail in Klutho Park. The city cannot deny knowledge of its existence. Only governmental authority could have set such an official cone at each end of the surface. Those cones can protect no humans from the glowing hirsute trapezoids breeding in that oil. I am sure you have many concerns pulling you in many directions, but glowing hirsute trapezoids crawling up from a giant oily surface and devouring biker after biker sounds like a disaster for both our city and your poll numbers.

(TO THE HEAD OF RESEARCH AND DEVELOPMENT AT EA GAMES)

This morning I found my daughter and her boyfriend slack on the living room carpet, eating Lucky Charms and watching a YouTube clip of an unknown human in another state or maybe another country playing a video game in which a scantily clad woman force-feeds a sex toy to an elderly gentleman until his throat clogs and he expires. The police drive through a wall, shoot her in the head, and rape her corpse.

Although I have reflected on this matter for several hours, I still cannot say which role the human was playing.

(TO THE HEAD OF RESEARCH AND DEVELOPMENT AT GENERAL MILLS)

You will be unsurprised to learn that my daughter and her boyfriend are among the subset of humans who eat only the marshmallows of their Lucky Charms.

Also: I have eaten our home's remainder of black worm marshmallows.

(TO THE GENERAL MANAGER OF PETSMART STORE #3571)

Is it possible that two conscious humans of whatever condition of mind could eat Lucky Charms, watch a YouTube clip in a living room, and fail to register the death funk of a rat purchased from your store?

(TO THE PRESIDENT OF THE UNITED STATES)

I doubt you have been briefed on the funerary practices of rats. Internet reports distinguish a pack's consumption of a dead rat from human cannibalism. These reports explain that the survivors eat the deceased out of fear that a corpse scent will draw predators to their cage.

(TO THE MAYOR OF JACKSONVILLE, FLORIDA)

Flashes of YouTube misery dance across the eyes of humans who share a peculiar condition of mind. In the flashes I see glowing hirsute trapezoids dragging a scantily clad woman under a depthless oily surface. I see a rat king patiently eating the stomach of the corpse of the President of the United States in a section of the sewer system below the bike path running through Klutho Park. Please act to prevent these visions from becoming reality.

(TO THE GENERAL MANAGER OF PETSMART STORE #3571)

I have carried the uneaten remainder of the defective rat with me into my daughter's bedroom and under her bed. It has leaked the last of its organs stickily into my palms and shirt. Black worms have slunk up from my stomach into my red plastic heart. I am waiting to discover who or what will find us in the dark. I await any and all advice.

BESTIÄREN / THE BESTIARY

/ Brendan Allen

ÄNGARNA
Dog

▶ Your child
     the sleeping dog

  needing to feel afraid

▶ Also available in:
  panda

BERGLUBB
22 oz gray

▶   don't risk
              the
        proof.

DYNAN
white

▶ Two

  clean
  ones

▶   up to 8
  in the space between

▶   quickly create

▶   wide
and shallow
space

FJÄDRAR
off-white

▶The duck
feels fluffy

              excellent
▶

neck.

GODDAG
black / white

▶The runner

           creates a

set

GULVED
green

▶   is
durable

▶   is strong

    more beautiful

▶

dark blue,

    design

SANELA
dark green

▶ velvet
color
soft to the touch.
▶
easy to remove
▶
dark gray, dark red

SMÅSPORRE
Queen

▶
in a
soft hollow
▶ their
ability
to breathe

throughout the night.

SÖTVEDEL
Queen

▶ soft
down
▶
a warm
environment
▶ if feel
cold
▶
a temperature
that
kills

ROSENDUN
Queen

▶ A

     protector

▶

         store and
release

        rises,
    , and   drops

VEKETÅG
Queen, gray

▶

        a ruffled
texture.
▶   soft
  spread

[unidentified]
15 oz round

▶   storing
        grains,
   and nuts.

[unidentified]
25 oz square

▶One

    perfect for

         sing

CONTRIBUTORS' NOTES

Brendan Allen is a recent graduate of the Temple University MFA and teaches writing as an assistant professor at Trine University. His work has recently appeared in *DIAGRAM*, *Prolit*, and *Voicemail Poems*. He's also the developer of *CentoQuest*: A text-based, choose-your-own-adventure, poetry-writing video game. You can play it here: https://bibliomancer.itch.io/centoquest.

Colette Arrand lives in Athens, Georgia, where she is a writer, an editor, and a publisher. She is the author of the poetry collection *Hold Me Gorilla Monsoon*, as well as the non-fiction chapbook *To Denounce the Evils of Truth*. Through Fear of a Ghost Planet, her zine press, Colette distributes a number of self-published works.

Mary Biddinger's stories have appeared in *DIAGRAM*, *Gone Lawn*, *On the Seawall*, and *West Trestle Review*. Her current project is a flash fiction novella that chronicles the adventures of two graduate school roommates living in Chicago in the late 1990s. Her most recent book is *Department of Elegy* (Black Lawrence Press, 2022). She teaches at the University of Akron and in the NEOMFA program.

Gabriel Blackwell is the author of seven books, the most recent of which are *Doom Town* (Zerogram Press, 2022) and *CORRECTION* (Rescue Press, 2021). He lives in Spokane, WA.

Coleman Edward Dues is the associate content producer at the Academy of American Poets, where he produces *Poem-a-Day*. His recent work can be found in *Word For/Word*, *Ligeia*, *Blazing Stadium*, and *petrichor*, among other places. In New York, they call him Tex.

Bradley J. Fest is associate professor of English and will be the 2022–25 Cora A. Babcock Chair in English at Hartwick College. He is the author of two volumes of poetry, *The Rocking Chair* (Blue Sketch, 2015) and *The Shape of Things* (Salò, 2017), and recent poems have appeared in *Dispatches from the Poetry Wars*, *Pamenar*, *PLINTH*, *Verse*, *Version (9)*, and elsewhere. He has also written a number of essays on contemporary literature and culture, which have been published in *boundary 2*, *CounterText*, *Critique*, *Genre*, *Scale in Literature and Culture* (Palgrave Macmillan, 2017), and elsewhere. More information at bradleyjfest.com.

Lillie E. Franks is a trans author and teacher who lives in Chicago, Illinois with the best cats. You can read her work at places like *Enchanted Conversations*, *Poemeleon*, and *Drunk Monkeys*, or follow her on Twitter at @onyxaminedlife. She loves anything that is not the way it should be.

Day Heisinger-Nixon is a poet, interpreter, and translator. Their work has appeared or is forthcoming from *Peach Mag*, *Boston Review*, *Foglifter*, Ugly Duckling Presse's *Second Factory*, and elsewhere. They are currently based in London.

Nora Hikari (she/her) is an Asian American transgender poet and artist based in Philadelphia. Her work is published or forthcoming in *Ploughshares*, *Washington Square Review*, *Palette Poetry*, *Foglifter Press*, *The Journal*, and others. Her chapbook, *GIRL 2.0*, was a Robin Becker Series winner and is available at Seven Kitchens Press. She was a finalist for the 2021 Red Hen Press Benjamin Saltman Award, and can be found at her website norahikari.com.

Emily Wallis Hughes grew up in Agua Caliente, California, a small town in the Sonoma Valley. These poems are in the manuscript of her second full-length book. Emily is the author of *Sugar Factory* (Spuyten Duyvil, 2019). You can read her poems in *Berkeley Poetry Review*, *Blazing Stadium*, *Elderly*, *Prelude*, and many other literary magazines. Emily teaches undergraduate creative writing courses as an adjunct instructor at Rutgers–New Brunswick in New Jersey. She and Jason Zuzga are the editorial directors of *Fence*. You can read more about her work at emilywallishughespoetry.com.

Callie Ingram is a PhD candidate at the University at Buffalo. Her poems have appeared in *P-QUEUE*, *Dream Pop*, and on Poets.org (as recipient of the 2021 Dan Liberthson Poetry Prize). Her scholarly work is published or forthcoming in *Critique: Studies in Contemporary Fiction* and *American Book Review*. Find her on twitter @callie__ingram.

Sal Kang (they/them) is a writer, editor, and translator living in

New Jersey. They strongly believe that hard cookies are superior to soft cookies.

Born in 1987 in Seoul, Kim Ha-ri majored in journalism in Kook-Min University and now works at a factory. Her work has appeared in the Korean web magazine *D5NZ5N*, the independent Korean poetry magazine *Wege*, the quarterly Korean literary magazine *Epiic*, and *McCoy's Monthly*.

Marcus Pactor's new book is *Begat Who Begat Who Begat* (Astrophil Press). His first book, *Vs. Death Noises*, won the 2011 Subito Press Prize for Fiction. His story "Megaberry Crunch" was selected for *Best Small Fictions 2021*. His work has most recently appeared in *3:AM Magazine* and *Juked*. He lives and works in Jacksonville, Florida.

Simon Perchik is an attorney whose poems have appeared in *Partisan Review*, *Forge*, *Poetry*, *Osiris*, *The New Yorker*, and elsewhere. His most recent collection is *The Gibson Poems* (Cholla Needles, 2019). For more information, including free e-books and his essay "Magic, Illusion, and Other Realities," please visit his website at www.simonperchik.com.

David Welch is the author of *Everyone Who Is Dead* (Spork Press, 2018) and a member of the core faculty of StoryStudio Chicago. His poems in this issue of *Always Crashing* are English-to-English translations from Jack Spicer's *After Lorca*. Visit him virtually at www.davidwelch.me.

Cajetan Sorich is a writer and performance artist who grew up beside a soybean field in Illinois. Her work has appeared in *Scapi Magazine*, *MAKE Literary Magazine*, *Queen City Writers*, and *Open Heart Chicago: An Anthology of Chicago Writing*.